Freddie, Bill and Irving

By Paul Bennett

Trafford
PUBLISHING™

Order this book online at www.trafford.com/08-0534
or email orders@trafford.com

Most Trafford titles are also available at major online book retailers.

Illustrated by: Kate Shannon
Cover Design by: Kate Shannon

Note for Librarians: A cataloguing record for this book is available from Library
and Archives Canada at www.collectionscanada.ca/amicus/index-e.html

Printed in Victoria, BC, Canada.

ISBN: 978-1-4251-7692-1

*We at Trafford believe that it is the responsibility of us all, as both individuals
and corporations, to make choices that are environmentally and socially sound.
You, in turn, are supporting this responsible conduct each time you purchase a
Trafford book, or make use of our publishing services. To find out how you are
helping, please visit www.trafford.com/responsiblepublishing.html*

*Our mission is to efficiently provide the world's finest, most comprehensive
book publishing service, enabling every author to experience success.
To find out how to publish your book, your way, and have it available
worldwide, visit us online at www.trafford.com/10510*

www.trafford.com

North America & international
toll-free: 1 888 232 4444 (USA & Canada)
phone: 250 383 6864 ♦ fax: 250 383 6804
email: info@trafford.com

The United Kingdom & Europe
phone: +44 (0)1865 487 395 ♦ local rate: 0845 230 9601
facsimile: +44 (0)1865 481 507 ♦ email: info.uk@trafford.com

10 9 8 7 6 5 4 3

To my Father, Ken Bennett.

Prelude – 1955

A FEW MILES inland from the Sussex coast, on a hill that overlooks the surrounding countryside, is a rambling Victorian building much added to by huts, temporary buildings and dimly lit tunnel corridors that slope away from the main building like the tentacles of an octopus. This is the South Sussex General Hospital, quiet now, in the early hours of the morning, but in the maternity unit the lights burn bright and the post midnight shift is busy at work.

Mum had been in labour for over five hours and a birth was now imminent. Two midwives variously handed the gas and air mask to Mum, applied damp towels to her forehead, held her hands and made comforting comments and gently coaxed her through the trials of labour. They monitored her pulse, timed the contractions, and listened carefully to the babies' rapid heartbeats.

At ten past four in the morning twin boys came into the world. Mum was ordered to relax, while the babies were washed. Then, swathed in large white towels, they were placed in the arms of a damp, but radiant Mum. Dad was called from beyond protecting screens to see his twin sons. William and Frederick had been chosen as male names and the names were proudly uttered for the first time to their first- and second-born sons.

Dad sat on the edge of the bed alongside Mum, and the four of them had a few moments together despite the bustle of clearing away around them. It was then that a midwife observed Mum grimace. She rushed over with her stethoscope. Within seconds the midwife was calling for assistance. Another child was on its way, and within ten minutes another boy was being washed and swathed to join his brothers. The unit began to fill with doctors and nurses. Twins were rare, triplets a special event. Mum now held this third child close to her.

Dad was allowed back in again and his only concern was, "What are we going to call him?"

They had expected twins, planned for twins, but this third child had no name prepared for him. Dad spun around expecting an answer, but all eyes were on him. He glanced beyond the open door, into the corridor.

"This unit opened 12th May 1950," read the plaque on the wall, "by the Right Honourable Irving Steed MP."

"Irving," gasped Dad, as if being pressured by an interview panel.

"Irving?" said Mum, some surprise in her voice. "Irving," said Dad, resolved.

"Irving," said the midwives, porters and doctors, nodding approval but not absolutely sure why the name sounded so appropriate.

Alone with their three newborns, Dad asked Mum how they were going to cope. "Don't worry," said Mum, "we'll manage, together we'll manage."

However, five months later Mum was managing alone. Dad had run off with a seventeen-year-old waitress from a tea-shop in Peasmarsh. Mum seemed to show no great surprise at this, but was a little bewildered as to how Dad had got to know someone so young in Peasmarsh.

CHAPTER 1

TWELVE YEARS LATER

"YOU'LL NEED YOUR coat, it's bound to rain," Mum called out to Irving who was rounding the hall corner, stepping off the last step of the stairs.

As usual Freddie and Bill were ready in their coats. Mum was at the door, her hand on the latch, and Irving was in the middle of doing something else.

"Hurry up, dear, I can't be late again. Have you got your packed lunch?"

Irving, having half picked his coat from the pegs, dropped it and disappeared into the kitchen where his packed lunch would be in a bag on the side. Freddie and Bill looked ceiling-wards. They knew better than to say anything. One word from either of them would set Irving off on one of his tirades and then they would never be out of the door.

This was part of the normal routine for the summer holidays. Had it been a school day, things might have gone a little smoother. Freddie and Bill usually left for the short fifteen-minute walk straight after breakfast, which left Mum to focus her attention on Irving and get him out of the house twenty minutes later. However, even this was never ideal as Mum often had to retrace the journey to school when Irving had failed to arrive. Usually he was to be found en route chatting to one of the assistants at the cake shop, or helping the old tramp that frequented the local area to pump up his bicycle tyres or sharing breakfast with him. The tramp carried a cooking stove on his bicycle rack and had a pan hanging from the crossbar. He was known to set up on the roadside in any location to cook himself breakfast and Irving could never resist a second breakfast.

On another occasion Mum rounded a street corner to hear Irving's voice, but there was no sign of him. Irving was trapped in the middle of a privet hedge. A schoolmate had bet Irving that he could not lay on the top of the hedge as if it were a mattress. Needless to say, Irving had accepted the challenge.

During the summer months Mum had a job on the town pier. The kids had to spend the day near to hand and within Mum's contact. However, there was little that Mum could do to control the kids' behaviour, but at least she would not come back to a wrecked home or have to travel across town, after work, to drag the kids back.

The four of them arrived on the warm but breezy sea-front, Irving as usual some steps behind and still half out of his raincoat which did not look as if it would be needed after all. Mum drew them close, each in turn, and hugged them and planted a sticky kiss upon their cheeks.

"Be good for me, boys." This was her usual parting remark, and the boys chorused back, "We will."

Mum moved away with a shake of her head and that proud, purposeful step that she usually had when departing towards the pier entrance. The boys gazed after her until she disappeared from sight.

"Right," said Bill to Irving, "you sort out the stall and start getting it set up and me and Fred will go and get some stock."

This was their normal activity for the days of the summer weeks. They had a trestle table that was stored away in the ticket box office at the entrance to the pier, and the boys lugged it across the pavement from the pier entrance and sold from it whatever they could lay their hands on. The range was usually quite considerable because they scrounged, purloined and otherwise obtained whatever they could procure from the local shop owners. The boys were known throughout the town with a certain degree of notoriety, but also with a degree of understanding of their motives and because this had gone on for several years, sometimes even with a degree of affection.

Irving started to argue but Bill said, "It's your turn, Fred. Irv, you came with me last Friday and nearly caused the punch-up in Turner's bookshop, remember?" Bill and Freddie started off, leaving Irving struggling to recollect how he might have possibly have come to start a fight in a bookshop.

Freddie and Bill made their first port of call at Abrahams the grocers, just a three-minute walk from the pier. Mr Abrahams, in his apron behind the counter, looked up as the door bell jangled and the two marched in.

Mr Abrahams was the image of what you might expect of a small town grocery shop owner. Quite large, mid-forties, a little bit of a piggy face, a small, almost Hitler-like, moustache, spectacles and a mop of red hair going a browny grey at the edges. "Might have known it would be you lot. Nine oh three, and I haven't had my first sale yet and you'll be wanting something for now't. I haven't got much for you today, a few old packets of biscuits and you can have those jars of jam I've put on the side there."

The boys stared at Mr Abrahams, the beginnings of mock disappointment on their faces. Freddie had wandered over towards the sweet display by the door.

"You've usually got more than this for us on a Monday, Mr Abrahams," said Freddie.

"I know, but last week was a poor week and there is precious little stock that I can spare."

Freddie was now leaning into the big box that contained the large multi-coloured gob-stoppers.

"Now, leave those alone, lad." said Mr Abrahams. "You should know better than that. I can't sell goods that have been handled."

"If they've been used before they shouldn't be on sale at all," came back Bill, quick as a flash.

"You know what I mean," said Mr Abrahams, rising to the bait and getting flustered. He strode towards Freddie, who nonchalantly began polishing the gob-stopper he had taken on his sleeve and placed it carefully back in the box just as Mr Abrahams arrived before him.

"OK, Mr Abrahams, we'll take what you've got," said Bill, defusing the tension and putting the jam and the biscuits into an old carrier bag. Mr Abrahams huffed.

The two boys left the shop, leaving Mr Abrahams looking up and down the street in the vain hope of materialising a customer out of thin air. As soon as they were out of earshot, Freddie said, "Well, Billy boy, what extra did you get?"

Bill showed him the two tins of ham and a tube of toothpaste. "Never fails to work, the old one-two routine," said Bill, grinning at Freddie.

They continued in this fashion for about an hour, in and out of nearly all the shops near to the sea-front. Most of the shopkeepers were wise to their stunts and had bags ready to push into their hands before they could come into the shop. Even so, they managed to work an old routine at Evans the baker, where they claimed that their bag had split.

"Can't we just have an old bag or box to put our stuff in?" said Bill.

Mrs Evans was stuck between rummaging under the counter for an old bag or going out the back for a carton. Mr Evans was still working in the bakery section behind. "Keep a close eye on those two," she said to her husband as she dashed to the store cupboard at the rear. Mr Evans peered through the glass peephole to see the two angelically studying the shop's light fittings. His forebodings of mischief assuaged, he looked away for approximately ten seconds, in which time one cream horn was removed from a display of ten, one cream slice was taken from a display of six, and half a dozen chocolate and shortbread biscuits disappeared from a display tray at the rear.

Mrs Evans re-entered with a box. "Here you are boys, will this do?"

"Yes, that'll do great," said Bill. They left meekly, with smiles on their faces.

"Did you keep an eye on them, Joe, like I asked?"

"Course I did, love," said Joe taking off his overalls.

It was not until thirty minutes and several customers later that Mrs Evans became aware of gaps in the display that should not have been there, but by then she had been too busy to remember whether she had sold the cakes or not.

Shortly after ten o'clock they rejoined Irving, who was waiting impatiently in front of a table covered in green baize and with chalk boards in front proclaiming great bargains. Freddie and Bill were weighed down by the eight bags and a carton they carried between them.

"Looks like a good haul, bruvs," said Irving.

"Better than average," said Bill.

Between the three of them they started putting all of their goods on display. The more risky items which had been, if you like, obtained without the supplier's permission were either concealed at the rear of the display or kept back in the bags for later in the week. The setting-out of their wares was done in a professional manner with small paper and card signs that said what the items were. The only thing left off was the price. Rather like an upmarket jewellers or West End clothing store, prices on goods was considered bad form. The customers had to ask what the price was and since in the vast majority of cases the items had been obtained for nothing, they set a price they thought the customer could afford. If it was overpriced, they could cut the price or sometimes, according to their whim, refuse to sell an item.

"It's too expensive for you" they would say to local boys gathering around, or "not for sale at the moment" to some potential customer that had incurred their instant dislike. Sometimes they would give away. They acted like modern-day Robin Hoods; if the need was great, they could afford to hand over for free.

With all the day's wares and signs in place, they stood back and admired their achievement.

"Time for some free cakes," said Bill and got out the spoils of their visit to Evans.

Business was quite brisk. Many of the locals were wise to the boys' games and knew that a cheap but good packet of biscuits or tin of meat could be had at cutprice. Among frequent visitors were the pensioners out on walks from their homes and accommodation who knew that there were some good bargains to be had, and the boys usually always set a reasonable price for these regulars.

The local council with its trading standards officers and the local police turned a blind eye. Freddie, Bill and Irving were not quite savvy enough to realise the workings of local politics that placed around them an invisible protective ring against petty bureaucracy and law and order, but they took full advantage of the particular circumstances they found themselves in.

Freddie, Bill and Irving never questioned their mother's employment on the pier or wondered at how, since they were without a father, they seemed to manage quite well and never lacked for the basics in life. Sometimes the inkling of suspicion was aroused within them as during the course of the day several, always well-dressed, well-shod, upright gentleman with refined accents would wink or nod in their direction as they passed by or left the pier. The boys just accepted this as part of their natural standing in local society and politely accepted the affection and familiarity.

The boys usually got to see a good few of their school friends every day. Most were on good terms with the trio, since not to be could lead to problems in the playground, but they did have one or two enemies, one of whom was Marcia Stellings. Marcia thought that she was much too good for most of her school-mates. This was reinforced by the fact that her father was somebody "important in the City". Every morning he left the house at ten to seven to do the local commute to London, in league with those other gentleman who still sported pinstripe suits and bowler hats and furled black umbrellas with smart leather attaché cases.

Marcia was with a visiting aunt and together they stopped at the entrance to the pier. While her aunt fussed over change for admission, Marcia had walked over to the boys and cast a suspicious eye over the goods for sale.

"Where on earth did you get all this tat from?" she asked. Freddie was nearest to her and ignored her question. "Where," I said, "did you get this tat from?" Marcia repeated in a shriller, more accented voice.

"From the same good supplier that your father gets his underpants from," said Bill. The other two brothers started to crease up.

"I beg your pardon," said Marcia, now pretending that she had not heard and now embarrassed since her aunt was moving nearer.

"I repeat," said Bill, raising his voice, "from that same fine emporium that supplies underpants to the nobs of this world."

Freddie and Irving had fallen beneath the table and could be heard writhing and gasping in mirth beneath it.

"Whatever is going on?" asked the aunt.

Marcia had gone bright red. "It's these pathetic boys," she said. The aunt looked disdainfully at the boys through her thick-lensed glasses.

"I don't think that these are the sort of people that you should be mixing with Marcia. Come along." The aunt strode off and Marcia turned, still red-faced, to Bill.

"Your mum's on the game. I expect that's what she's doing right now down on the pier."

Bill, for once, was speechless. As Freddie and Irving picked themselves up and brushed off the dust, Bill looked angry. "I'm not having her say things like that about our Mum. We are going to sort her and her uppity family out."

Freddie and Irving exchanged puzzled looks. "What did she say, Bill?" asked Irving.

"Never you mind. We are going to sort this one out."

Lester Michael Stellings was a man of routine, was a man of stature, was seem-ingly man of substance, and also was somewhat of a fraud. True. he worked in the

City, true he had an office job, and true that he worked in and among many of the big corporate names of the City, but his job was that of a lowly office clerk. Once he had arrived at the rather grand offices where he was employed, he took the lift to the fourth floor, walked to the end of a long, dismal and damp corridor, took out his key and opened the office door. Therein he monitored and requisitioned stationery supplies. His suit jacket, bowler hat and umbrella went on the coat stand, not to be collected until the clock hands were upon five o'clock. His wearing of a pinstripe suit and bowler was laughed at by other colleagues, but Lester had been there such a long time that most ignored him and took him for just an eccentric.

Any money that Lester had was the remains of a legacy left him ten years before by his aunt and now reaching perilously low levels.

Something would soon need to be done, but for the moment, the pretence continued.

Lester was a man of routine and always rose at six o'clock so that he could bathe, shave and take breakfast in that order. At six forty precisely, he would leave the house and walk ten minutes to the station before catching the six fifty train.

Cynthia Patricia Stellings was a woman of ambition, a woman of morals and a woman with standards. She had urged Lester to take a partnership in his company. Little did she know that the chief porter was more likely to become a partner than Lester. She wanted a larger house, in a better, more upmarket area of the town, further away from the beaches and the sea-front and the ghastly weekend and holiday trippers who arrived from the London suburbs every season in steadily increasing numbers. She had her heart set on a detached house in a leafy lane alongside the golf course on the edge of the town, just a few hundred yards from the next resort with its tasteful tea-shops and antique stores.

Cynthia was determined to model Marcia in her own image. True, there had not been much choice over primary school, but once secondary school choices came up, if they were living on the edge of town, they could consider a good grammar school or even a private school.

Cynthia had put all of her efforts, her determination to refine, into their current home. The house was immaculate, inside and out. The rooms were not cluttered, furnishings were tasteful, if not expensive, and the carpets were the very best they could afford. The lawns outside were mown, flowers in the beds and the borders carefully edged. The garden fences were new and the gate was painted a glossy black with the number in large silver digits. Unfortunately some of the neighbours did not live up to the same high standards and Mrs Stellings would gaze disapprovingly at their cracked gates , unmown lawns and straggling flower beds as she passed by.

The morning had gone by quickly. Mum popped out at lunchtime to check on the boys. She bought them each an ice cream and gave them some slices of cake wrapped up in individual bags. She chatted with them at the stall and then made her way back on to the pier to eat her own sandwiches. The afternoon was generally the busiest time of day as people came out for their after-lunch and afternoon walks. Many would stroll on the pier and would use the boys' stall as a source of food and refreshment, rather than pay the higher prices on the pier.

The summer afternoons could get hot. Sometimes the boys erected a canopy over the whole stall. In turns, one of them would serve while the other two would doze, eat ice creams or read a comic beneath. Looking up behind them they could see the tops of the buildings that led up and away from the sea-front and see the heat haze rising from the baking roofs.

George Robinson had retired from the police force on the rank of inspector at the age of fifty-two after thirty-five years of service working in the Lewisham area of south-east London. He had planned to travel round the country in a camper van that had been purchased some years before, but his wife had fallen ill in the few years before his retirement and had passed away in the weeks before the end of his job. So he was alone, but by no means old and no family to speak of living in his local area.

George wanted a new life, a new location and possibly a new relationship, but the latter could wait. He chiefly wanted to forget all those wasted years when the job had been his life and he and his wife passed hours together at weekends and during the erratic vacations. The rest was overtime, more cases, more duties. He had known the station sergeant better than he had known his wife. No joke intended. Now it was all past and all too late.

He had made the decision to move to the south coast, a small resort with a social life, not too far from the old manor so he could go back for the reunions and just to get back into the 'smoke'. He got withdrawal symptoms from being out of London for too long. He could not pinpoint what it was – the long rows of terraced housing that went on up and down in serried ranks towards the horizon, the bustle of the streets, fag ends on the pavement, the eternal twilight of a London night, being known, being recognised, the smell of beer outside the pub door, the smoke filled rooms, the smell inside a London bus during a rain storm, probably all of these things. They were the things that mattered to him. Made George Robinson who he was.

Nonetheless he made the move. Sold the house, didn't want to buy a new one straight away, and moved into nice residential accommodation, a few pounds a week, just a few roads back from the sea-front.

Four months later he had met Mum, Lillian, during an afternoon stroll along the pier. George had found it harder to meet new people than he had anticipated. There was not quite the same natural easygoing-ness that existed in south London. In the pubs he was treated as a stranger and although he had struck up odd conversations, most of the time he ended up drinking alone, which was not what he wanted.

George could not face tea dances or afternoon bingo. He had popped into several of the hotels along the front in order to strike up conversation, but the residents seemed shy, already had their circle of partners and friends, or in George's opinion were too feeble or frail or uninteresting to be worthy of attention.

Mum had been taking a lunch break away from the kids and had some sandwiches open on her lap and was gazing out to sea. George had walked up, raised his hat and enquired if he might join her on the bench.

"Yes, please sit down," said Mum, "there's plenty of room."

George sat down, quiet for a while and then looking sideways said, "If you don't mind me saying so, you've packed yourself a fine lunch."

"Would you like one?" said Mum, offering the pile of sandwiches across. "There are ham and pickle on the left and egg and cress on the right."

"That's kind of you," said George, "but I've just had a snack in the café on the front. Don't let me stop you enjoying your lunch, though. I expect you have to be back at work soon."

"I work on the pier," said Mum, "so I haven't got to rush."

"Really," said George, "I didn't think there was much employment on the pier."

Mum turned to take in George more completely. George noticed Mum's change in attitude and interest and was immediately attracted her strong face and smile which he had not fully appreciated when he had first sat down.

"You must be new to the area," said Mum. "There are four little businesses half way down the pier, a glass artist, an ice cream, rock and postcard shop, the clairvoyant, though most of the time that's closed, and the tattoo studio."

"Are you telling me that you work as a tattoo artist?" asked George, genuinely amazed. Mum looked directly at George, he was quite taken aback by the intensity of her stare and he thought he almost detected a flirtatious smile on her lips.

"Come back with me in about fifteen minutes and I'll show you what I do."

They chatted about this and that while Mum finished her remaining sandwiches. They got on to George's former job as a policeman and his plans for retirement, thrown into ruins by the untimely death of his wife, and then Mum stood up and George walked with her down the pier.

She was a good deal taller than he had expected, taller almost than he, and the way she walked, with a haughtiness something like the girls to be found around Lewisham station in the late summer evenings. But no, it could not be possible, he must be mistaken.

The afternoon's business had turned out to be sluggish. After a brief spurt of activity around three o'clock there was only slow trade. A lot of people came to look, poked and prodded, opened and turned over the items on display. The boys took turns at serving, about twenty minutes on and forty off.

They played a game, while not dozing, of guessing who the people were from the shoes, trouser legs and skirt bottoms that they could see beneath the green baize that covered the stall.

"Boring old fart," said Irving, "with hairs sticking out his ears and a 'tache."

"Nope," said Bill, "bald head and sticky-out ears like a windmill."

"Bet yer ten bob," said Irving.

"Bet yer a quid," said Bill.

"Yer on."

"Yer on."

They heaved themselves up behind the stall where Freddie was relieving the punter of a handful of silver. The man was in his sixties, thin and stooped, and with a few sweaty hairs pasted across his scalp.

"See – bald. I win," said Bill. "No way," said Irving, "look at the 'tache and there's more hair coming out of his ears than an Orang Utan."

"I beg your pardon," said the old man, taking in the gist of the exchange. "Do you always insult your customers in this way?"

"This is no insult," said Bill. "If you want insults, we can give you plenty. We was just having a bet. In fact you can settle it for us. When you go to the barbers, do they singe your ear hairs?"

The old man looked astonished. "I beg your pardon?"

"When you go to the barber's," said Bill, "do they burn the hairs sticking out of yer lug 'oles?"

"This is disgraceful," said the old man to another customer that had just turned up. "You come to give them some trade and all you get in turn is rudeness."

"I'm not being rude," insisted Bill. "We are just trying to settle a bet."

"I'm not getting involved in any bet," said the old man. "You young 'uns should show more respect for the elderly and your customers."

"He's right," said Freddie. "Your bet has lost the stall money."

"Give over," said Bill. "If you'd been under the stall instead of Irv, you'd have done the same."

The old man and his companion began to wander off grumbling and muttering.

"That's about it then for today," said Freddie. "We better get sorted away."

They began to take apart the stall, putting unsold items into the boxes behind the stall and shifting the table over to the pier box office.

They were nearly cleared away when Mum appeared with a man alongside her. The three boys looked up again in case the appearance of the man with Mum was a coincidence and he would turn off in another direction. However, the two of them kept heading straight for them.

"Who's he then?" muttered Irving under his breath.

"How should I know?" asked Bill.

"Looks like one of Mum's types," said Freddie, "but I've not seen him before."

Bill looked again as they came towards them. From behind his hand he whispered to Irving, "He looks like trouble, looks like a copper."

Mum and George stopped before the three boys. "Finished for the day, then?"

But the boys' eyes were on George. "This is George," said Mum. "I met him earlier today. He's going to come back with us for some tea."

The boys exchanged glances. "Who are you then?" said Irving, full of his normal subtlety.

George looked at Irving and began to say something, but Irving carried on. "Bill says you're a copper. Have you come to keep tabs on our business?"

George smiled. "Bill's right, I was a copper, but I'm retired now and I'm not interested in your business, so long as it keeps you occupied and your Mum happy."

"That's alright then," said Bill, "but what are you coming back to tea for?"

"That's enough, Billy," interjected Mum. "He's our guest and we are always polite to our guests."

Bill and the boys went quiet at this and tagged on behind Mum and George as they walked back the house.

Tea was really the evening meal and Mum had quickly put together some ham, sausages, eggs and beans that were quickly demolished by the boys and the remains mopped up with slices of buttered bread. The meal had taken place nearly in silence with George and Mum talking quietly between themselves. Bill was finished first.

"Is it alright if we go and play next door?"

"So long as you don't make too much noise and you clear the supper things back into the kitchen first."

The boys took their plates and other items off the table and disappeared into the kitchen.

"What's he up to?" said Freddie to the others.

"Don't know and don't really care," said Bill, "so long as he's not keeping an eye on us. Anyhow we've got work to do. We're going to get even with Marcia Stellings."

"I'm not even sure what she's supposed to have done," said Freddie, "apart from being her normal snotty self."

"She slagged off our Mum," explained Bill. "She said that she was on the game."

Freddie and Irving stood open-mouthed at this explanation, neither of them entirely sure of all that it implied, but both of them sure it was something pretty bad.

"I've had an idea," said Bill. "Them Stellings are so up themselves in their own importance that we're going to take them down a peg or two in the estimation of their neighbours. We're going to make up a big banner and hang it across their roof so that when they wake up tomorrow, everyone is going to know about where the Stellings live."

They decided that they could not risk being overseen in the back room so they went down to the shed to make up the banner. Freddie had asked Irving to get some old sheets out of the laundry cupboard, but what he brought down looked suspiciously like new sheets. They stitched the sheets together to make something about thirty feet in length and ten feet wide. Rope was attached to the corners and two smaller cords at the centre to attach it to the chimney stack. The slogan they carefully printed out in six-foot-tall, bold black letters. It took them two hours' work and they left it spread out to dry.

The plan was to go to bed as normal and set the alarm for about five o'clock so that they could go to the Stellings' to set it up. There was some argument about whether they should hoist up the banner in the early hours, but Bill had insisted that the morning was best; the banner might get seen if it went up too early and someone might alert the Stellings. His way meant that the banner would only be seen as neighbours opened their blinds and set off out of their houses for work.

Mum brought the boys up some hot chocolate just after ten o'clock as they were getting ready for bed. "You're very quiet tonight, boys," she said. "Is there something going on that I should know about?"

"No," said Bill for the three. "We're just knackered after a long day."

"So long as it's just the result of an honest day's work, then," said Mum with a wink.

The boys slept fitfully in the knowledge that the alarm under Bill's pillow would ring in the early hours. When it rang, the three were up and into their clothes in a few minutes and then creeping out the back door, down to the shed where they folded up the banner and put the ropes in separate bags. They went out the back gate and up the back alley-ways towards the Stellings' house. It was just beginning to get light. They spotted a couple of dog walkers heading towards the front, but apart from that the area was deserted.

There was no other way into the Stellings' back garden apart from through the front gate and over a wooden side gate adjacent to the house. On Bill's orders they stayed low, but, of course, Irving had to drop the bag with the ropes to the ground with a thud.

"Shut up, for God's sake," said Freddie. "If they're light sleepers, they'll be looking out of the window and then we're blown."

"That was hardly noisy," Irving began to remonstrate, "I ..."

"Shurrup, you pillock," said Bill. "You're like a bloody foghorn."

"I'm no bleeding fog ..." started Irving again.

"Quiet! Hit the deck," said Bill, and as they did so, a window in the top of the neighbouring house was opened. Bill was laying on his back and through a chink in the fence could see a tired face looking up to the road. They lay there in silence for what seemed an age before Bill said, "It's OK, let's go."

They left the front gate open so that the clank of it closing to would not wake the Stellings, and scuttled down the side path. Irving was given a leg-up so that he could release the top bolt on the reverse of the gate to the side passage, and the three passed through and into the back garden. Here they had the cover of medium-height shrubs and small trees. The garden seemed dark and quiet compared to the front of the house. The boys started to roll out the banner and Bill looked up for the best way to scale the back of the house.

Lester Stellings had slept badly. He always slept poorly these days. As a boy and a young man he had always slept soundly the whole night through, but as he became older a good night's sleep had become more and more elusive. Often, at dawn, he lay there shattered, craving his return to bed the following evening when once again he might attempt a decent night's unbroken sleep. Now he lay half awake waiting for the alarm to go off. He had been further troubled by noises that seemed to come from the rear of the house and the roof, but it was probably pigeons, or more likely seagulls. It was getting light now; he could see the increasing light seeping in from behind the blinds. Next to him his wife slept the sleep of the innocent. Lester felt that one aspect of his sleepless night was the increasing guilt he felt over misleading his wife over his job. He had never sought advancement, never sought to ascend the slippery pole of promotion. In fact his job, dull, trivial and mundane as it was, remained a secure position and one that many might remain proud of.

His sin was to have mislead his wife into supposing that he had a more important, more influential and better paid job. The savings that he relied on to boost their income were all but finished and within the next month or two they would be living on considerably less. Lester knew something had to be done, but he was not sure what and least of all how to go about doing it. The alarm sounded, he stabbed at the off button and wearily moved his feet onto the carpeted floor.

Marcia loved her sleep. She loved the dreams that came with it. She could not understand her friends who spoke about nightmares and bad dreams. All her dreams were good. Often she dreamed of her friends, her parents, her school which were down below her as she floated in the sky. She had the ability to levitate and in her dreams she always wondered why others did not have the same power to float and rise up above their problems.

Marcia was used to being woken up by her mother at around seven thirty. She would be brought up a cup of tea which was placed on her bedside table. Cynthia Stellings would gradually draw her from the clutches of her last fleeting reveries and would wake her to a smile. Marcia had never known any other way of waking and in her bed she slept these final minutes of innocence.

It had started well. Irving had gone up the drainpipe like a monkey. A rope was attached to his belt and as he reached the point where the pipe connected with the gutter, he easily leaned over the edge of the roof and pulled himself on to it. A few low, crouched steps and he was on the ridge tiles and then across to the chimney stack. He put the long rope around the base in a noose and then lowered himself to the edge again to hall up the sheet which Bill and Freddie had already spread out. This was taken to the front of the chimney and then rolled out on the other side. Two weights in the bottom corners ensured that the sheet stayed flat and Irving tied the small cords around the chimney base to make sure it was all secure. It looked fine to Irving from his position and he waited until Freddie came into view giving the thumbs up to confirm this.

The last stage was to get quietly off the roof so that the three could admire their work from across the road. The arrangement was for Irving to be lowered back down by the other two from the ground, the rope going around the stack. Three backward steps down from the edge and he would be on the ground. Freddie and Bill took up the slack and slowly released the rope as Irving went over the edge.

Lester was in the shower. This for him was the best part of getting up. He would come out refreshed and more alive. Again he was vaguely aware of unusual noises around him but he put them down to the boiler thumping, or perhaps Cynthia had gone downstairs. He wrapped a towel around him as he left the steam of the shower and began running the sink tap for shaving water. At the same time he threw open the bathroom window and this was when an unusual shadow caught his attention. He looked out again and the shadow grew from above until feet, legs, body and finally face moved past the window.

"Morning, Mr Stellings," said the face.

"What the ..." returned Mr Stellings and looked beneath in the direction the face had gone.

At this point Irving realised he had left a bag on the roof. He signalled to Bill that he needed to go back up again and the two hauled back to bring him back to the roof. Irving passed Mr Stellings at the window once more.

"Morning again, Mr Stellings," said Irving.

Mr Stellings was flabbergasted, who was this boy drifting up and down past his window offering good morning greetings and what the hell did he think he was doing? No sooner was this thought thought, than Irving appeared once more on his way back down.

"Nice day, Mr Stellings."

Lester Stellings tripped over the edge of his towel as he ran to the bedroom for some clothes.

Irving reached the ground and Freddie and Bill pulled to bring the loop of rope off the roof. However, the pulling and the weight of Irving had forced some of the rope under the lead flashing at the base of the chimney and into a crack in the cement made by wind rain and sun. Pull as they might the rope would not loosen. Irving saw the problem and joined the two to pull. Unfortunately they were not aware of the considerable leverage that they were applying to the chimney stack. The first few clatters of loose cement on the tiles should have given a clue and then certainly the first red brick that skittered noisily down to the gutter. But they were too intent on having their rope back and their nervousness made them pull even harder.

The catastrophe began with a roar as several bricks bumped and bounced down the roof and then skipped through the air to plunge through the broad glass panes of next door's conservatory to shattering effect. The roar became an avalanche as the whole chimney stack began to split in two, chimney pots, bricks, cement and coal dust falling evenly on both sides of the house.

The trio legged it out of the side gate as the din continued with bits of chimney and broken roof tile still falling. They ran up the bank on the opposite side of the road to survey the scene.

Long afterwards they each admitted that they could not have orchestrated a more apocalyptic scene. Brick and tile dust still rose in the calm air and descended from the roof. The strong rose tinted rays of the dawn sun were exaggerated like search-light beams by the descending dust. The front garden was a mass of tiles, bricks, shattered chimney pots and mangled rose beds. Neighbours were at their windows and doors. The postman had stopped to gawp, letters in hand, the milk-man paused mid-stride, bottles in hand, to survey the scene. The lady out walking with the two Great Danes was wiping her glasses in disbelief and now behind all this the banner could clearly be read: "Now open: New Council Rubbish Dump".

Freddie turned to Bill. "I think that we might have overdone things a little, don't you?"

Irving turned to hear Bill's reply, but Bill just grinned.

CHAPTER 2

FREDDIE, BILL AND Irving never made it back home and into bed that morning. Half way home, as they ducked and dived through back alley-ways, a police car pulled across the gap in front of them. They turned to run off the other way, but two burly policemen blocked their exit. They were unceremoniously dumped into the back of a police van, their shouting, swearing and banging to no avail, and whisked off to the local police station.

Three hours later, after they had sat glumly in separate cells, they were unlocked and brought into a large interview room. Mum and George sat on one side of the table, the triplets sat together and a gruff sergeant sat at the other end.

"If it was down to me," started the sergeant, wringing his hands and then placing his palms down on the table, "and if you were a couple of years older, we would be going for charges that would put you all in Borstal for a couple of years. As it is, you're lucky lads. My friend Mr Robinson here," he nodded towards George and Mum, "has persuaded me to be lenient and that's despite all the damage that you've done."

Freddie, Bill and Irving exchanged glances. Freddie spoke up.

"Actually, most of the damage was an accident. All we wanted to do was put up a banner."

"I'm surprised that you've got the nerve to speak," said the sergeant. "Everything that has happened is the direct consequence of your actions. Mr Stellings wants me to press criminal charges to try and get some compensation for the damage that has been done to his house and his garden. However, as I said, because of the intervention of Mr Robinson, we've decided that things can be dropped if you are all out of circulation for the rest of the summer."

The boys looked at one another. "What's 'out of circulation' mean?" piped up Irving.

"He means that we've got to stay indoors," said Bill, miserably.

"No, actually, that's not what has been agreed," said the sergeant. "Your Mum and Mr Robinson will explain fully, but you're all going away from the area for the rest of the summer."

The boys looked aghast. "But we can't leave Mum on her own," said Freddie.

"We're not going nowhere," said Bill.

"That's right," added Irving, getting to his feet. "You can't make us."

"Boys," said Mum, speaking for the first time. "This is going to be for the best. There's going to be a lot of local gossip and comments made. If you stay with me, there will be more trouble, and I can't afford it. To save you going to court, I'm going to have to pay compensation to the Stellings."

"Compensation," Bill almost shouted. "Those stuck-up snobs shouldn't get a penny off us. They got what they deserved."

"This is exactly," said Mum forcefully, "what I meant. If you stay here, this is going to go on and on. And it's not. This is where this all stops. I'm paying compensation to keep you out of more trouble and you're going away to your aunt's for the rest of the summer."

"What aunt?" said Bill. "We ain't got no aunt that I've heard of before."

"She's a cousin of mine and therefore your aunt. She lives in Scotland, in a quiet town where you won't be able to get up to the sort of trouble you've been in here. Tomorrow morning you're on the train to Scotland and you'll be there for four weeks. You can write as much as you want and you'll be able to phone me a couple of times a week."

The boys looked flabbergasted. There were so many questions that they wanted answered that they could not think fast enough to get them out.

George spoke up. "Thank you, Sergeant Vickers. We'll make sure everything goes as agreed. Hopefully the rest of the summer will be a bit less eventful."

The boys looked downcast as they trooped out of the interview room, through the reception office and out into the bright sun.

"Bang goes our summer," said Bill.

"Yep, all we've got to look forward to now is haggis and chips," said Freddie.

"And men who wear skirts," said Irving.

The journey to Scotland was intended to be uneventful. Mum said goodbye to the boys at home and they each carried a suitcase out to George's car. The journey up to London took place in almost total silence. It was only when they reached the Thames that the boys began to brighten up and start to notice the landmarks and the city people on the streets.

At Euston George took the car through a side entrance and right up to the platform. A train guard that George knew was going to look after them up to Glasgow and from there they would be taken by bus to Helensburgh by their aunt.

The train was already at the platform, one of the longest the boys had ever seen. The locomotive pulling the train was out of sight, beyond the curve of the platform, and there was intense activity as coaches were cleaned and provisioned for the journey. The boys were to sit in a carriage next to a large guard's van. Unusually the first-class compartments were at the rear of the train, followed by the restaurant cars, the guard's van and then the rest of the second-class accommodation.

George introduced the boys to Mr Roberts, a short, bald headed man in his forties, with a permanent serious expression and very thick-lensed glasses in black frames.

"This is going to be a bundle of laughs," said Freddie in an aside to the other two.

The boys said meek hellos and put their cases at the side of the guard's van.

"That way you'll have more room in the carriage, and you'll need it for a journey that will take over six hours."

Mr Roberts showed them their seats, told them to make themselves comfortable and went back into the van to help load some more crates.

George produced some packets of sweets, the packed lunch bag that Mum had made up and some comics. "Behave yourselves," said George, "if not for me, then for your Mum." Then he was off and the boys sat on their own.

Irving stared glumly out of the window where a railway worker worked on a train on the next track.

"Bugger this for a game of soldiers," said Bill.

"We've got to lose Goebbels next door or were stuck on the most boring train journey ever invented," commented Freddie.

Irving was still gazing out of the window, then he turned to his brothers. "I think I have an idea. You make sure that baldy thinks I've gone off to the toilets long term, tell him I've got a gippy stomach or something."

With that Irving climbed off the train and disappeared. He went round to where the railway worker was still working on the other track. Irving stood still watching for a few minutes. Eventually the rail worker looked up.

"Interested in trains are you?"

"Too right," said Irving. "I want a job on the railways when I'm older."

"Come over here then, I'll explain what I'm doing."

The railway worker showed Irving how he was decoupling carriages, how he opened the connection and also released the service cables between the carriages.

"These carriages are going to be shunted down the line to be cleaned later," he explained. "Not a difficult job? Eh? Just need the right tools and it's a five-minutes job. I'm off for my tea break now. Where are you going?"

Irving thumbed at the Scotland train.

"Oh aye, Scotland eh? You're settling for a long trip. If you want a job on the railways, make sure you apply as soon as you can. It's a job for life and the pay's not too bad."

The man climbed off the tracks and made his way across the platform towards the staff canteen. Irving saw the tool box where the man had deposited the decoupling tools, opened it, picked up the tools and jumped down on to the track by the Scotland train.

Irving was back in the carriage twenty minutes later. "Was I noticed?" Irving enquired.

"Nope," said Bill, "he was too busy loading up. We should be off in ten minutes. What did you do?"

"You'll find out soon," said Irving with a grin.

The guardsman checked on the boys about five minutes later.

"You all prepared? If I was you, I would get my head down for a couple of hours. There be nothing much to see until we get beyond the Midlands."

The boys feigned compliance, curling up in their seats and making themselves comfortable.

The train left the station with a final slamming of doors, whistles and several jerks as the diesel pulled away.

It took five minutes. Baldy came rushing into the carriage on the way to the front of the train. He looked in a panic. The boys raised inquisitive eyes.

"Bloody hell," he said, "we've left the first-class carriages back in the station. There's going to be hell to pay." He scurried off like an overwrought mole through the carriages.

The boys grinned together. "We won't see him for a while," said Bill.

"Teach the first-class passengers to expect special treatment," added Freddie.

One of the irate first-class passengers to be left marooned on Euston station was a certain Mr Lester Stellings. Lester was now without a job as a consequence partly of the boys actions, but mostly because with his late arrival in the office, another manager had gone through the supplies requisition books and found what appeared to be gaping errors. In fact the errors were less the result of financial impropriety and more that of the idiosyncratic way in which Mr Stellings went about recording stock orders and disbursements. However, Mr Stellings was asked to take leave while the books were properly investigated and Mr Stellings, being in a rather inflammatory state of mind, told them that if they did not trust him then they could stick their job. The firm had accepted his offer.

Mr Stellings' marriage remained in place by the slenderest of gossamer threads and his relationship with his daughter was also at a very low ebb.

Lester did not tell his wife about the loss of his job, merely that he had to go away for the firm for a few days and since that suited her very well, nothing more was said. Lester blamed Freddie, Bill and Irving entirely for the misfortune to him and his family. He was livid that as a result of some deal between their mother's friend and the police. they appeared to have got off without proper punishment and he was determined that true justice was going to be meted out to them. He learned about their departure to Scotland and he was set to follow them. He had allowed himself the one luxury and privilege to travel first class and enjoy a meal on the journey. Now that would not be happening, damn and blast British Rail. At least he could not blame this on the boys.

The trio used the departure of the guard to explore the train. A corridor ran throughout and most of the compartments were full. The guard was obviously up with the driver using the telegraph relay to organise the reconnection of the first-class carriages. After exploring the length of the train, they returned to the guard's van to see what treasures had been stored there. Mostly it was trunks and large crates but there were also bicycles, fishing rods and two large cages that obviously had some sort of creatures within. They looked more closely and peered through the closely nailed slats. There was little light, so it was difficult to see within.

"They're birds," said Irving, "dozens of them, little brown things."

"Probably grouse," said Bill. "They'll be taking them up to the moors to be released."

"What for?" asked Freddie, puzzled.

"They shoot them; the twelfth of August is the start of the shooting season."

"Poor little blighters," said Freddie. "I think that we should do the decent thing and let them go beforehand."

"Well, we better wait until the train stops," said Bill. "We can't let them out while its moving."

"What is the first stop?" asked Irving.

"Crewe, ain't it, Bill?" asked Freddie.

"Yeh, I think so, and if I'm right, it'll be a long stop because they'll be bringing up the first-class coaches from behind."

The boys took themselves back to their seats and curled themselves up again. It wasn't too long before the guard came back and saw the trio, apparently asleep. They're not going to be the trouble I thought they might be, he thought to himself. He had too many other concerns on his mind. It wasn't totally his responsibility to have checked the train before it left, but he should have noticed that the electric services were out in first class. In fact one of the passengers had asked him why the lights were out. There were going to be some uncomfortable questions asked of him before the end of the day.

The train slowly heaved itself into the great junction that is Crewe station. As the train shuddered to a final, screeching halt beside a platform, the guard made a tannoy announcement that the train would be on the platform for up to thirty minutes while carriages were reattached. He then disappeared off to the station office to find out the progress of the diesel shunting the first-class carriages back up the track.

"This is our chance," said Bill. "Irv, you have a scout around the station, see what's worth having. Fred, you keep a look-out for Goebbels and I'll get those cages open."

Bill clambered onto the cages to find an opening handle, or at least a door, but there was none. He realised that he would need some tools to get the cage open. He looked around the guard's van for something he could use, but there was nothing he could see of use, so he set off after Irving to find something he could use.

Crewe is one of the biggest railway junctions in the country. There are twelve platforms and apart from being part of the mainline London to Scotland route, there are connections there for Wales, Cumbria and the north-west as well as to the eastern side of the country and the Midlands. In mid-summer, when the Scotland-bound train pulls in, platforms are a hive of activity, passengers waiting to join the train and passengers moving from one platform to another, people piling cases on and off trolleys, people making their farewells or greetings, couples hugging, couples kissing, smiles growing, tears streaming, children spilling around, porters being questioned, porters pointing, porters directing. For a few minutes the place is a chaos of activity until the trains pull out, and momentary peace returns until the cycle begins anew.

Bill went out into this chaos. He soon saw a box marked safety equipment and nobody noticed as he removed a crowbar and a small axe from it. He tried to catch sight of Irving, but he had long disappeared off into the crowds. When Bill returned, Freddie was still waiting at the door. He gave the thumbs-up sign to Bill. Bill whispered to Freddie, as people waiting to have items loaded were beginning to wait alongside the guard's van.

"Keep the door closed and put anyone off who tries to put stuff on, tell them to wait for the guard."

Bill set to work on the cages. He did not want them to look as if they had been broken open; he hoped that he might leave the appearance that the cages had moved and cracked. He found a seam in the wood that he could split with the axe-head, then he used the crowbar to extend the split right down to the floor. He realised as he was doing this that there weren't just birds on the floor of the cage but birds on several levels. Each cage must hold hundreds of birds. Bill finished his work on one cage. The noise was deafening as the birds became agitated, squawked, shrieked and rushed around in the cage. Then Bill worked on the second cage in the same way. He left the openings so that with one pull he could tear off the side of the cage.

Bill crossed to the door and looked out. "What's it like out there, Fred?"

"Not too bad at the moment. Most of them have wandered off to find the guard. You'd better hurry; he'll be back in a moment."

Bill went back inside and returned to the door after thirty seconds. "Come on, Fred, leg it."

He closed the door firmly shut behind him.

Just at this moment, the first-class coaches were being shunted onto a spare track alongside the main train. The journey had not been easy for the passengers, bumpy, slow, with frequent stops, and no leisurely breakfast that they had been waiting for. One of the passengers, Colonel Carstairs Carruthers, had travelled on this line to the family Highland estate, man and boy, for over sixty years. Never in his life had he been so inconvenienced. He had taken solace in the liberal supply of malt whisky that he carried with him, which partly compensated for the lack of an extended breakfast. He had fallen into a sleepy stupor, much to the relief of his long-suffering wife and travel companions, but as the train pulled into Carlisle, he began to wake from his sleep, half believing that they were already in Scotland.

There was a queue of about ten people with assorted items of baggage waiting by the guard's van door, when a very red faced and puffing guard arrived. He heaved aside the long door to the van and could not believe his eyes as a surging, squawking, heaving mass of brown feathers flooded onto the platform. The young grouse did not fly but acted as a leaderless pack of lemmings, surging as a mass along the platform. Women shrieked, children tried to catch individual birds and railway staff tried to shoo and usher the birds into some invisible safe haven.

This din was heard and the sight seen by Colonel Carruthers as he heaved himself to his feet. He looked, looked again, rubbed his eyes and exploded, "Grouse, grouse, damned bloody grouse, they're everywhere."

And with that, an instinctual response took over. He grabbed his gun case from the luggage rack, broke the rifle, inserted two cartridges and began firing at the birds while the train still edged along the spare track.

If the scene was already one of total chaos, it now became one of total panic as more women and children shrieked and screamed, porters hit the ground and the grouse finally found wing and as a mass ascended into the air as a dense brown cloud. The firing continued into the sky, children howled, women wept and the police were called.

Lester Stellings had a seat behind the Colonel and still dozed as the train pulled in to the station. The first massive report of the shotgun brought him to his senses. He did not know what was happening, an IRA bomb?

He could smell the cordite, he could hear the screaming, then a second great bang and smoke billowing over his head. He looked over to see the crazed eyes of Colonel Carruthers as he ejected the spent cartridges. He took in what was going on.

"You can't do that, man," he shouted. He saw Mrs Carruthers cowering in her seat, unable to act. "Look, we're in a station, there are people around."

Colonel Carruthers swung the barrel away from the window to level it at Lester's head. "Damned pacifist are you?" roared the Colonel. "See those birds, they've got to be shot, there's hundreds of them. If we don't get them now, they'll take over the country."

With that he turned back to the window and let off another shot. Lester knew that he had to do something fast. From the look of the other passengers they were either going to do nothing; some could conceivably be joining him. He lent across to the Colonel and grabbed the barrel of the gun, the Colonel pulled the trigger and a shot blasted through the station roof.

"You've got to stop," shouted Lester.

"I'm not stopping now," shouted the Colonel. "This is the best day's shooting I've had since Ypres in '16."

Lester struggled with the Colonel now that the gun was empty. The Colonel pulled away, dragging Lester over the seat. With Lester's grip loosened, the Colonel went for new cartridges. Lester brought himself to his feet and began to struggle with the Colonel for possession of the gun. They pulled backwards and forwards like two kids fighting over a toy. Finally Lester had the strongest grip and fell backwards on to the floor, gun in hand.

Of course, this was the precise moment at which uniformed officers charged into the carriage from both directions, throwing themselves on Lester, seizing the gun and handcuffing him in the same move.

As Lester was led away, not one person, uttered a word to remonstrate. It was as if they all instinctively knew that he did not have the stamp of a true first-class passenger.

The train was a whole hour late when it left Crewe station. The guard, was even more red faced, perspiring and jittery than ever. He had been formerly told by a senior rail manager to "get a grip and do his job properly". Formal disciplinary action was a distinct possibility. When he finally got out of his van, the boys, who he had almost forgotten, were sleeping like logs, as if the whole pandemonium had passed them by. Irving had returned to the compartment, bag in hand.

"A complete station toolkit," he had exclaimed.

The train crept on towards Preston and Carlisle. The boys were actually quite subdued. They played cards, and as the train came into Preston station, they raised their heads as the train drew in alongside the platform. Almost exactly opposite them on the platform stood two large policemen, Irving almost gulped and the three of them immediately started to feel extremely nervous, until they noticed that the policemen stood either side of an even larger man, rough shaven, short brown hair, wearing navy overalls. He was handcuffed to both of them.

"He's a prisoner," said Bill. "He is obviously being escorted to a gaol further up the country."

"How do you know he's going to another prison?" demanded Freddie. "He could just be on a visit, to a funeral or something."

"True," said Bill, "but it's probably a bit late in the day for just a visit. I think he's being moved."

"Whatever he's doing, he don't look too happy about it," chimed in Irving. "Wonder what he's inside for?"

"Dunno," said Bill, "but I think that we should make it our business to find out."

Lester faced three hours of questioning at Crewe Police Station. Finally, they seemed to believe his story. The Colonel would be intercepted at Glasgow on arrival, and providing they could get some witness statements, Lester would probably go free. They required a contact address in Scotland, which he gave, and they took him to a quieter Crewe station so that he could continue his journey. Lester was shattered; he felt ill. He had hardly eaten since early in the morning, he'd had a lukewarm mug of coffee at the police station, he felt on edge, he felt a nervous wreck. He was beginning to wish that he hadn't started this quest for revenge.

Papers were handed over to the guard by the policemen and their prisoner started to move up the train. Freddie gave them a few minutes to get ahead and then followed them up through the train. They had found places round a table about five carriages further up. One policeman sat next to the prisoner, still handcuffed, and the other moved to the opposite side. Freddie put himself on the other side of the dividing seat and waited. After about twenty minutes the policeman sitting on his own went off to get some coffees. Freddie took this chance to look over the seat. Both the prisoner and the policeman appeared to be dozing. Freddie crept around the corner of the seat so that he was next to the prisoner, but partly hidden from the policeman. He cupped his hands to his mouth.

"Hey, hey." Not a movement. "Hey, hey," again.

The burly man whose head had slipped down so that it was nearly on the armrest opened one bloodshot eye.

"Push off, kid," he said.

Freddie did not move, the eyelid closed and then opened slowly again fifteen seconds later.

"You still here? I told you to buzz off."

"I only wanted to ask," said Freddie. "Me and me brothers saw you come on at Preston. We just wondered what you'd done and whether we could help."

"I murdered someone, and I'll be doing the same again if you don't push off."

Freddie did not budge. "We might be able to help out."

"How can you help out," said the prisoner, "when I'm bleedin' handcuffed to this rozzer?" He nodded at the dozing policeman.

"We've got tools," said Freddie, "bolt-cutters, wrenches, saws, hammers, you name it we've got 'em." The man's eye opened slightly wider. "Wot you goin' to do then, bring 'em up here and cut me free while the filth looks on and has a cup of coffee?"

"I'm sure you could think of something."

"I already have," said the prisoner. "Get the tools up to the toilet compartment at the end of this carriage, use something to pull down the panel over the cistern, leave the gear and put the panel back again, then leave the rest to me."

The prisoner expected the boy to rush off. "Wot you waiting for then?"

Freddie looked him in the eye. "What do we get out of it?"

The prisoner smiled, revealing broken and steel-capped teeth. "Canny little urchin, aren't you? You get me off this train and I'll see you alright. Is my word good enough for you?"

Freddie nodded and disappeared back to his brothers.

Bill and Irving were waiting anxiously for Freddie's return.

"Well," said Bill, "what did you find out?"

"Not a lot, except he's trying to get away."

"That's pretty obvious. Do you know his name, where he is going, what he's done?"

Freddie glumly shook his head.

"What the hell were you doing up there all that time then?" asked Irving.

"It was difficult, I had to whisper, he gave one word answers, but I said we could get him some tools."

"You did what?" exclaimed Bill.

"He suggested that if we had tools we could leave them in the toilet cubicle and he'd do the rest and see us alright."

"The problem with that," said Bill, "is we know nothing about him. If he's just nicked something or clobbered someone, fair enough, but what if he's some psycho that's going to slice someone up for no reason the minute that he gets free?"

"I never had the chance to question him properly about that," said Freddie embarrassed. "He said he was a murderer but I think that he was just joking."

"Bloody great," said Bill. "We've done some capers in our time, but freeing a murderer will cap the lot. Anyway if we've made a promise, we'll just have to go ahead and hope it goes for the best. Irv, you take the tools up to the cubicle and I'll give him the signal that they're in there. We'll have to keep close tabs on him after that."

They had to work fast. They had reckoned that once the train got near Carlisle that the prisoner would not be able to leave his seat. Irving stuffed the tools into the top of his trousers, covered them with a coat and Bill followed him up to give a signal to the convict. Then the two of them stood by the window just beyond the cubicle to see what would transpire.

After a few minutes the prisoner came along with a police officer who removed the handcuff from himself and placed it on the prisoner's free wrist.

"How the hell am I going to use the toilet like this?" demanded the prisoner.

"I'm sure you'll manage," growled the officer.

The convict disappeared inside and the policeman took up a position outside the door.

Although just out of the policeman's view, Bill and Irving clearly heard the clunk as the bolt-cutter sliced through the handcuff chain with ease. The policeman had heard something too.

"What's going on?"

The reply came back, "I just slipped."

"Hurry up," said the officer curtly.

The door opened and the prisoner came out with his hands together, and the officer bent to unfasten one handcuff in order to reattach it to himself. As he did so, the prisoner swung forwards with his forehead, a Glasgow kiss. The officer's knees buckled and he slid to the floor. The prisoner took the keys, quickly unlocked both manacles and then lifted the large policeman to his feet with ease. The toilet door was kicked open and the policeman placed upon the seat inside. The convict looked at the boys by the window, gave a thumbs-up to them and disappeared up towards the guard's van.

Bill and Irving looked back to see the other policeman still in his seat and then followed the convict back towards the end of the train. Freddie was surprised to see the convict arrive.

"Where's the guard, son?" the convict demanded.

Freddie nodded towards the van. "He's still in there as far as I know."

The convict looked cautiously around the door and could see the guard dozing in his seat. He crept forward and quietly moved a couple of suitcases from a pile. Moving them into the boy's compartment, he wrenched them open and started to look for items of clothing that he could wear. He soon found a tee shirt, jeans and a hat which were swiftly changed in to. He stuffed the discarded clothes back into the cases and put them back on the pile, keeping out a few papers that he shoved into his pocket.

At this point Bill and Irving arrived back in the compartment.

"What are you going to do now?" asked Bill.

The train had reached the outskirts of Carlisle and was beginning to slow. The prisoner pointed towards the door.

"Out there, as soon as the train has slowed enough."

The prisoner rummaged in his pocket and took out some scraps of paper. He handed a card to Bill. "Thanks, boys. I can't do anything for you now, but you can contact me later."

Bill responded with a torn-off strip of cigarette carton. "This is our address in Scotland."

With that the convict turned to look out of the train again; it was crawling alongside a steep embankment. The door was flung open and the convict disappeared.

Bill pulled the door shut, looked at his brothers and then at the card in his hand.

"What does it say?" said Freddie.

"Torchy and a London phone number."

"Torchy," repeated Freddie, "what sort of name is that?"

"Dunno," said Bill "but I'm getting a bad feeling about this."

A few minutes later the other officer came thundering into the carriage.

"Have you seen him?" he shouted. The boys looked up, feigning puzzlement.

"Who's that?" said Irving.

"Our prisoner. You must have seen him; the other passengers saw him heading this way."

"We've been dozing," said Freddie. " I think someone went into the guard's van."

The policeman moved through and the boys could hear the splutters as the guard woke up and the policeman's angry questioning. He came back in.

"Are you certain that you saw nothing? The guard says he saw no one come through, though he probably would have slept through it anyway."

Bill said, "I didn't see anyone."

The policeman looked at him closely. Bill could feel his guts begin to tighten.

"What's that you've got in your hand, son?"

Bill went cold; he could feel his heart thudding because he knew he still held the card in his hand. He thought fast.

"I found it on the floor at the end of the carriage."

"When was that, exactly?" said the policeman taking the card.

"A few moments before you came," said Bill. "I thought I heard something bang."

"This is his. He must have dropped it before he jumped off the train."

"It says 'Torchy' on it." said Bill, "Is that his name then?"

"Torchy, that's his nickname; the bloke's a nutter, an arsonist. Part of the reason why he's being moved is that he set fire to his wing at Leicester Prison and now he is on the loose again."

The guard came back into the compartment.

"We are going to have to make an official report on this as soon as we stop in Carlisle," the policeman said to the guard. "The other officer's been knocked out in the toilet. The whole thing is a shambles. Somebody has helped this prisoner escape and I think they are still on the train. We'll have anyone who leaves the train at Carlisle picked up for questioning. The rest will have to wait until Glasgow."

The train was slowing to its final halt at the station. The guard started to move up along the carriage with the policeman. The boys were left alone.

"That was a close one," said Bill. "I thought I was for the chop."

"What's all this arson business then?" said Irving.

"He sets fires," said Bill. "I thought that as soon as I saw the name. He's probably a murderer as well, he's probably burned people alive if he's set buildings alight. We've done it now. It's down to us that he's on the loose. A few grouse are neither here nor there, but this bloke's different. We'd better get our thinking caps on to try to put this right."

"Thing is," said Freddie, "he could have gone anywhere. What about that number, do you think that will give us a contact?"

"We could try," said Bill, " but for the time being we better lie low. If they find the tools in the toilet, they are going to know that he was helped and they will be asking awkward questions of anyone that moved around the train."

The train was stopped for another forty-five minutes at Carlisle while police got on and off and started to search in compartments. The train eventually departed to complete the last leg of its journey.

It was early evening before Lester Stellings finally got on his train from Crewe. Worn out by his ordeal, he collapsed into his seat and fell into a deep sleep. It had become dark by the time his train reached the outskirts of Carlisle. The slowing and clattering of the train as it crossed points raised Lester to a state of wakefulness. It was a case of déjà vu. That same oddness as when he had been shocked by the report of the gun from slumber this morning. Something was not right, but as yet he could not be sure what it was. It had become dark, the low lights were on in the compartment. Those around him variously slept, read or tried to gaze out of the windows against the reflection of the inside lights. Those that were gazing, seemed to be in conversation, as if there was something to see.

Lester put his face close to the windows and cupped his hand against his head to shield the light. He could see the town ahead, but was it a festival or something? All around there appeared to be bonfires. He could see five or six of them; perhaps it was some local celebration. Then as the train drew closer to one of them, he saw it was a building in flames, and a fire crew was in attendance, and as they drew into the station and doors and windows were opened, he could hear the sound of sirens screaming close by and in the distance, and also the smell of smoke.

Eventually his train pulled away from Carlisle station towards his intermediate destination of Glasgow. Lester mused, what was happening to him? What was happening to the world? For years he had followed the same routine, the same orderly life, yet in a few days it had all seemed to have been thrown into chaos, his home wrecked, his marriage in tatters, his relationship with his daughter teetering on a precipice, shot at by a crazed colonel, arrested, and now as he left the borderlands of his country he might believe that the whole country was alight, sliding into a state of anarchy.

CHAPTER 3

FEW TRAINS HAD received such an extensive welcoming committee at Glasgow Central. As they pulled into the platform, the whole length of it seemed to be lined by police, with one or two on the opposite platform for good measure. The groups alighting from each carriage were escorted to different parts of the station to be questioned by detectives. As the boys overheard from a senior officer, never in his experience had so many criminal activities been perpetrated in the course of a single train journey.

The boys got off lightly. With a favourable report from a visibly shaken guard, they were asked a few questions, details were provided of a contact address, and they were taken to the front of the station.

Mrs Callaghan was waiting for them. She was a quite large, friendly and motherly woman, with a mass of curly red hair under a blue hat. The boys were quite taken aback as she greeted each one of them in turn, hugged them and kissed them upon their cheeks.

"Welcome to Scotland," she said in a strong, shrill accent. "You will be hungry after such a long journey so we will stop and get a meal first and then get the bus home."

The boys were soon to recognise that Mrs Callaghan had something of an obsession with food and mealtimes. The boys were ushered into the station buffet, sat down at a table and served up with large steak and kidney pies, gravy and peas with as many cups of tea, lemonade or fizzy orange as they could drink.

The boys had lost their tongues; even Irving sat quietly and munched his way through the pie. No sooner than they were done, a dessert was served up that looked like chocolate pudding in a chocolate sauce. Mrs Callaghan went off to 'powder her nose'.

"There's two sides to this," said Bill. "We're not going to die of starvation, but if we carry on like this, we're not going to be able to move in a couple of days."

"What I want to know," started Freddie, "is how we are going to play this. Are we going to stick it here for three of four weeks or are we going to get back south again?"

"And," said Irving, "what about this Torchy bloke, are we going to do anything about him?"

"I think a council of war is what's needed," said Bill. "We'll wait till we get where we're staying and then decide what our options are. The problem at the moment is that we have no cash and if we do want to run back south, then we'll need at least a coach fare."

"We could hitch," said Irving.

"Good idea," said Bill, "but it would take for bloody ever and we'd have to split up 'cos nobody's going to take three hitchers together."

At that point Mrs Callaghan turned up.

"Ready, boys?" she beamed at them, "Or are you still a little peckish?" Irving looked expectantly at his two brothers.

"No thanks, Mrs Callaghan. We've had plenty," said Bill.

"Well, we can't have you calling me Mrs Callaghan all summer. Call me Deidre."

"They've all got weird names up here," said Irving in an aside to Freddie.

Mrs Callaghan led them round to the coach stop. They waited about twenty minutes before a long cream and red coach turned up showing Helensburgh Pier on its destination board. They trooped on with about twenty other passengers, and so began the long journey out to the west of Glasgow, across the Erskine Bridge, through Dumbarton and on up to Helensburgh. The boys mostly stared out the windows and Mrs Callaghan read her book. After passing through Dumbarton, the road followed beside the Firth of Clyde and then the Gare Loch. The boys observed the dark, steel-grey waters and the low leaden clouds and thought how much unlike the south coast this all was. Eventually the first signs for Helensburgh were seen and the boys' interest increased as they drew into the edges of the town. Most of the buildings seemed very big, some seemed to have turrets like a castle, most of them seemed to be built of the same grey and pink stone.

The bus came to stop by the pier.

"This is it," said Mrs Callaghan. The boys hauled themselves and their bags off the bus and they looked out towards the water.

"This ain't no pier," was Freddie's first dismayed reaction to the stone promontory that stretched out in front of him. "Where are the stalls, where are the amusements and shops?"

It all seemed very bleak. One or two metal shuttered booths stood on the length of the pier, with a lone fisherman at its end.

"I don't know what you're used to," said Mrs Callaghan, "but its what we've got here. You can catch boats to the other side of the Clyde and down into Glasgow from here, and there is a fair here in early summer."

Bill and Freddie eyed the scene with the same sense of dismay as Irving. Individually they thought, if this is their idea of a pier, what was the town going to be like?

"It's only a short walk from here," said Mrs Callaghan, "so pick up your bags and we'll be there in no time."

Mrs Callaghan's idea of a short walk did not coincide with the boys' notion. For a start it was uphill, for another, they had bags while Mrs Callaghan didn't and the slope seemed to stretch on forever. They thought that at any moment Mrs Callaghan must turn up one of the long front paths, but she went striding on until they reached the brow of the hill and another uphill stretch reared before them. By this time Mrs Callaghan was twenty-five yards ahead.

"Do you need a breather?" she asked of them.

"I thought you said it was a short walk," gasped Bill, "not a trip up a mountain."

"Ach, you youngsters," Mrs Callaghan laughed. "I'll take you for a real walk tomorrow."

Another long street later, she stopped ahead of them in front of a tall house. It looked like all the others with its reddish pink stone and attic windows. The front garden was long and very neat with border flowers and a strip of mown lawn. Rather like the Stellings' garden before their reconstruction work, thought Bill. The boys were let into a long, well-lit hallway with lots of mirrors, a coat stand and other furniture. There was a thick red carpet, it was warm inside and the house smelled of polish.

"Here we are, then," said Mrs Callaghan. "Leave your bags in the hall and come into the dining room for a cup of cocoa. Then you can meet my husband, William, and then get off to bed."

"But it's only half past seven," piped up Irving, looking at the hall clock.

"It's early to bed, early to rise in this house," said Mrs Callaghan.

"But what about the telly?" said Freddie. "We always watch the telly in the evening."

"I'm afraid we have no television here, much to our shame, being the birthplace of John Logie Baird, but the reception is too poor. We listen to the radio instead."

"No telly," echoed Freddie mournfully.

The boys were led into a dining room where they were seated around a table. Presently the door reopened and a tall middle-aged man wearing a bottle-green waistcoat with a chain watch at the pocket came in.

"Hello boys," he said. "I'm William Callaghan, lord of this estate." Freddie's jaw nearly dropped but Bill saw the twinkle in the man's eye. "I hope you're going to enjoy your stay here. We've arranged an itinerary for you so you don't get bored and up to the tricks you have been at home. If you want to read there are plenty of books in my library and tomorrow evening there is a concert on the radio. I'm sure you're going to enjoy it here."

With that he walked out. Mrs Callaghan brought in a tray and a plate piled high with hot crumpets. She too disappeared again, leaving the boys dumb in dismay.

Irving was the first to regain his power of speech. "What the, where the ..., are we back in the middle ages? No telly, she blamed it on some Logie whatsit or other and Lord William and his library is expecting us to listen to a concert tomorrow … Bog off … I'm getting out of here."

"Calm down," said Bill, "we've only just got here, the food's OK, we've got to suss out the lie of the land and plan our moves. If we run back south again, we'll just get put back on the next train back or worse. I've got the feeling that William is not as bad as he seems, it's just a wind up to catch us off guard."

"It had better be," said Freddie, "otherwise four weeks up here is going to seem like a life sentence."

Irving was still stammering in his outrage. "B … bloody library. I've not read a book in three years. If he thinks the highlight of our day is going to be picking out books …" He was cut off as Mrs Callaghan came back in.

"I'm taking you up to your rooms," she said. "Two of you will have to share, and one can be on his own."

She guided them and their luggage up two flights of stairs. Compared with home, the rooms were immaculately laid out with patterned bedspreads, tied-back curtains, washstands with jugs and basins. On each bed there was a new set of pyjamas and a dressing gown. There was a chest of drawers in each room with a vase of fresh flowers.

Irving looked around. "This is a tart's room," he said.

"I beg your pardon?" said Mrs Callaghan.

"He means girl," explained Bill quickly.

"'Tart' isn't an expression we use here, young man," said Mrs Callaghan curtly. "Whilst you're under my roof, you'll remember your manners."

"Yer, 'll," was all Irving managed to get out before he was kicked by Bill.

"Button it," Bill indicated with a finger pressed to his lips. Irving fell silent.

Mrs Callaghan put Freddie and Irving in one room and Bill in the other, wished them good night and a sound sleep and pulled the doors to.

Freddie and Irving left it fifteen minutes before going over to Bill's room.

"I'd expect him to be in here by now," said Irving. He went to open the door, but it was locked. "The door's bloody locked," said Irving.

They tried the window, but that too was sealed.

"Let's face it," said Freddie, "we're well and truly kippered. We'll get some shut-eye and sort things out in the morning."

"Spose so," muttered Irving, "but I'm not reading no book."

Lester Stellings awoke to a new world, but not that of the previous night. He was in a very agreeable bedroom, the sun pierced through chinks in the curtain and he felt the luxury of clean linen and the smells of coffee and breakfast coming in from the hallway. Having arrived at Glasgow late at night, he had given up the idea of further pursuit of the boys and had taken a room in the station hotel. He had slept well and now felt that he had a new understanding of what had befallen him. The Sussex coast now seemed to be part of another world, and the daily commute part of some other person's existence.

Perhaps he should give up his pursuit of the boys, for they were only boys and part of a prank that had got out of hand. He could get another job, they could move, another town would bring new beginnings for all of them. Perhaps they could move right away, up here, into Scotland, enjoy the open spaces, the fresher air. This must be it, there was a reason why all this madness had happened.

After speaking to the police and being interviewed at length by detectives, Mr Roberts, the train guard, went to clock off from his shift. He was handed an envelope by a stony faced station manager. He knew what it would be and as he descended the steps from the gantry office, that was placed behind all the platform and destination boards, he tore open the envelope. "You are required to attend the railways disciplinary board on Tuesday 10th August." That was next Tuesday. He was angry and frustrated. Twenty years' loyal service and not a blemish on his record and then more mishaps in one day than one would expect in years of service. There had to be more behind this, an explanation for all that had happened. It had all been too fast, too continuous, this was his first opportunity to reflect.

He went down on to the platforms and asked some crew where the train had gone. Normally it would form part of another service back south, but given the criminal investigations it had been moved into sidings just south of the station. The guard made his way there. There were a couple of niggling suspicions at the back of his mind and he wanted just to make sure. He hitched a lift on a shunting wagon to the sidings and went on board the guard's van. There was no power now and so he had to use his torch. He examined the splits in the bird cages. They looked the same, but they didn't look very natural. He rummaged at the base of the cages, barging them with his shoulder to move them across. Then he found what he was looking for, an axe and a crowbar, and thanks to station bureaucracy they were both marked up in small white painted letters as to where they belonged, "Crewe". These had been brought onto the train at Crewe, exactly where the birds had been released. What had he done before this mayhem started? He'd made the tannoy announcement and then gone to the station office. Those ruddy kids, they'd heard the announcement, seen him get off the train and they'd nicked the equipment from a safety box. It could only be them; only they would have had the time. I've been had, he thought to himself, well and truly tied up and dumped upon.

If only he hadn't been lulled into a false sense of security by their pretence to be tired. If he was going down, so were they. He'd find out where they were staying from George and he'd hunt them down, if it was the last thing he did, he would.

"Torchy" Edwards had had the time of his life in Carlisle. Since a young kid he had been fascinated by fire. He was always buying boxes of matches. It never ceased to amaze him. You could start with a flame that could be cupped in the palm of your hand and quickly it could become an inferno, flames racing up into the sky, smoke billowing. He started with small cans of lighter fuel, he set fire to old cars, trees, garages, allotment sheds, anything with something in it to burn. He was caught from an early age too, told by police, magistrates and judges: "You may not set out to harm but your actions endanger life, divert fire-fighting resources from where they are needed. You will be responsible for manslaughter or even murder and then you will go to prison for the rest of your life." But he could not stop, and after increasing lengths of time in Borstal and prison facilities, the first thing he did on release was to start a blaze somewhere and then stand back and watch his handiwork.

As Torchy grew older so his pyromania grew more extreme. He needed treatment, but no one offered him the treatment that he needed. Brief psychological reports spoke of 'emotional deficit', 'an identification with the purifying power of fire', 'fire as gratification of a basic need'. One enterprising postgraduate had even begun a thesis based upon interviews with Torchy: 'Classical Pyromania and Jungian Primal Archetypes'. But the draft copy was found to be good kindling material and used to reduce another building to ashes. He was given his own probation officer on his most recent release from prison. Someone who had pleaded to work with him, because he knew the traumas that Torchy experienced, and believed that he could be reformed. However, the probation worker just turned out to be an apprentice pyromaniac who would willingly fill up jerrycans at the local petrol station before an evening out with Torchy. When questioned by a senior officer as to why they needed ten full jerrycans in the car boot when the main tank itself was nearly empty, he was unable to provide a satisfactory answer.

Carlisle had amazed Torchy in that it had so many derelict factories and warehouses. In little over two hours he had started over eleven fires in a ring right around the town centre. As the flames slowly subsided, he made his way back to the station, found a wallet on the floor and purchased an onward ticket to Glasgow. Arriving, just before midnight, and with his newly acquired wealth, he booked into the Glasgow station hotel.

The dawn of the new day arrived with an unusual luminescence formed by the combination of the high latitude and the low sun as it reflected off the water's surface and the surrounding hills. The boys opened their eyes and immediately recollected that this was their first day in their new home. Irving jumped out of bed and tried the door handle. It was open and as the door stayed ajar for a few seconds the heart warming scents of cooked breakfast drifted into the room.

"Looks like we've been released," said Irving to Freddie.

"Try Bill's door," called out Freddie, in reply.

Irving moved the few steps across the landing and opened Bill's door. Bill had evidently just awoken and was rubbing his eyes, sitting up in bed. "What's the time?" he asked of Irving.

"Dunno for sure, but it smells like breakfast is cooked."

"Better get some clothes on then and investigate."

The three of them pulled on some new clothes and pattered downstairs in stockinged feet.

They had half forgotten the geography of the house since their arrival the previous evening but were drawn along by the scents of the cooking. They arrived at the kitchen door to see Mrs Callaghan hard at work at the stove. She turned to see the three heads in the doorway.

"Good morning, boys. I hope that you all slept well and are hungry." The boys nodded. "Away then, to the dining room and I'll bring your food through."

The boys crossed the corridor to where she had gestured. The room was still rather gloomy, the curtains had not yet been drawn, and at one end of the table Mr Callaghan was sitting, paper folder in one hand next to his breakfast plate.

"You all slept well?" he enquired as they entered.

"Yes, except our doors were locked," said Irving.

"That was just to get you settled last night," said Mr Callaghan. "I don't suppose we'll need to do it again."

"No," said Irving. "It's not safe. What if there had been a fire?"

"We would have been straight up to your rooms if you had been in any danger," said Mr Callaghan. "As I said, it was only a temporary precaution."

"We're not used to locked doors," said Bill, "precaution or no precaution. At home we are allowed to go around the house free."

"Well," said Mr Callaghan, "I could give the easy answer and say that this is our house first, but I don't want to be unwelcoming. We'll agree that the doors won't be locked again."

"Sounds fair enough," said Bill.

The three sat and Mrs Callaghan brought in three steaming bowls of porridge. There was honey to go on top, tea to drink, then a cooked breakfast with black pudding, then a pile of toast with a choice of preserves: strawberry, cherry, peach, and also marmalade and honey. Thirty minutes later the boys could hardly move. Mr Callaghan was still reading his paper and had hardly seemed to have touched what was on his plate. Irving looked across.

"What did you have to eat then, Mr Callaghan?"

Mr Callaghan looked up from his paper. "Kippers."

"What, fish for breakfast?" exclaimed Irving.

"Aye, lad, fresh from the dock this morning."

"I've never heard of anyone eating fish for breakfast before."

"Well, you've missed out on a true delight, then," said Mr Callaghan. "Two kippers for breakfast sets you right for the day."

"Can I try some tomorrow?" enquired Irving.

"Course you can, boy," said Mr Callaghan.

Freddie and Bill exchanged glances. "Looks like he's going native," whispered Freddie from behind cupped hands.

Mrs Callaghan, who had not eaten with them, came in to collect the plates.

"I've got a programme set up for you today. This morning we'll take a walk over to Luss. We'll have a picnic lunch and then this afternoon I'll introduce you to some friends of mine and then we can walk the scenic route back home again."

"Not more walking," groaned Freddie.

"We walked miles yesterday," added Irving.

"Aye, well," said Mrs Callaghan, "walking's good for you; it builds your muscles, gets you out in the open air and gets you an appetite up. It also will keep you out of mischief, which is what you are up here to avoid."

"Yeh, we'd guessed that was what behind all these arrangements," said Bill. "We're not that bad really, just misunderstood."

"From what I've heard," said Mr Callaghan, "it's a little bit more than that. You've done a whole lot of damage and put your poor Mum under a lot of strain."

"Things got out of hand," said Bill, "but we were just trying to stick up for our Mum, any kids would have done the same."

"Nevertheless," interrupted Mrs Callaghan, "you're our responsibility now for the rest of the summer, and you will do what we ask of you."

"Fair enough," said Bill. "You've put your cards on the table, but we need a bit of free space for ourselves. We can't spend all of the next three or four weeks being trailed round Scotland."

Mr and Mrs Callaghan exchanged glances and then Mr Callaghan said, "We'll see how the first few days go and then if you've behaved, we'll give you some free time."

The boys were asked to go back upstairs and put on some warm clothes. A few minutes later they returned to the kitchen where Mrs Callaghan indicated to some big packages on the table.

"What are these, then?" asked Irving.

"Why it's your pack-up lunch."

"I thought we were going for a short walk," said Irving, "not a trip up Everest."

Mrs Callaghan smiled. "It never does to be without reserves, the weather up here can turn bad quite quickly. If it does we can find shelter and you'll be a lot happier if there is some food about."

"S'pose so," grunted Irving, begrudgingly.

Surprisingly for the kids, they set off out of the back door, down the garden and then up a sloping path that took them up towards the hills at the back of the house. They had walked about twenty minutes and the sun had seemed to have become a lot warmer. The boys began stripping off the jackets and pullovers and tying them around their waists.

"I'm baking," said Irving. "I'm never going to last out at this rate."

"I'm knackered as well," said Freddie.

"It's that breakfast that has done us in," added Bill.

Mrs Callaghan was several yards in the lead. "What's all the dissent in the ranks, then?" she demanded, turning back towards the boys.

"We're not used to all this early morning walking, that all," said Bill.

"Yeh," said Irving, "At about this time we're usually setting up stall by the pier."

"It seems to me," said Mrs Callaghan, "that this is how you get too much time on your hands. Another ten minutes walk and well stop for a few minutes at a neighbours. He's got something special to show you all."

Mrs Callaghan marched ahead again. Irving turned to Bill.

"They're all crackpots up here. How can it be a neighbour, we're bloody miles away from her house now?"

"Beats me," said Bill, with a shrug of his shoulders.

They continued a slow ascent on a path that wound back and forth, always appearing to be turning toward the back of a house and then veering away at the last moment. Finally they turned a corner and a large wooden gate stood before them.

"This is the entrance to Mr Alexander's property. We have to ask him permission to go further up the track, but we'll stop here anyway for as I said he has something to show to you."

Unlatching the gate they went past some screening trees and into the bottom of a large garden. The lower end of the garden seemed to be disorganised and untidy, but the top had neatly mown lawn and a table set out with a canopy over it. As they moved into the lower area the boys could see what looked like small wooden houses and they could see a figure in white, leaning into one of them. On closer inspection, the figure in white seemed to have a gauze veil hanging from his hat to half way down his body. He was holding something that looked like a small teapot which had smoke pouring out of it, and which he wafted across an exposed part of the small house.

The kids had already become aware of the buzzing in the air and had started swatting away the bees that frequently buzzed across their path.

Mrs Callaghan halted some ten yards before the first hive.

"Mr Alexander keeps bees," she explained. "He produces some of the finest honey in the area."

Freddie exchanged glances with Bill. "Is this going to be exciting, or what?" he said in an aside.

Mr Alexander had looked up from his work, returned the frame that he had removed from the hive, walked a few yards to a small table, put down the smoke can and taken off his protective hood.

Now the boys could see that Mr Alexander was a short, rather wiry man of about fifty five. He had white hair and an angular face, with thin lips. He had a very quiet voice and a strong Scottish accent, so that the boys found it quite hard to understand him.

Mr Alexander asked the boys if they wanted to see inside the hives. They were reluctant at first.

"We'll get stung to death, won't we?" asked Freddie.

Mr Alexander explained that honey bees were very reluctant to sting, unless attacked. Anyway, he had hats and veils that they could all wear, and as long as the boys did not become noisy and excitable, there would be no problem.

Properly attired, they all approached the first hive with Mr Alexander. He wafted the smoker across the hive vents and then began to withdraw a frame filled with honeycomb and clinging worker bees.

"The smoke makes them drowsy and unlikely to attack," explained Mr Alexander.

The boys came close so that they could see the activity of the bees. Mr Alexander explained that the hive was like a miniature city. He pointed out the different type of bee, female and male drones and then found the queen bee at the centre of the hive surrounded by its drones.

"How do they all know what they are doing?" asked Irving.

"A good question," said Mr Alexander. "They use chemical scents to communicate with each other. You just try and watch any one bee; they all carry out their individual operations, they're all doing individual jobs. Looking into a hive is just how looking at a town of humans must seem from space. Everyone is doing different things, going in different directions and it looks like chaos, but we're all going about our own business and there is a purpose in what we are all doing. The bees have a common goal, which is the collection of nectar, making honey and the survival of the hive."

The boys had listened intently and came up with a series of questions. In fact towards the end Mrs Callaghan wondered if it was still genuine interest or an attempt to avoid continuing the walk.

Mr Alexander lead them up into the upper garden where they took off their protective clothing and sat down for a drink of lemonade, which was brought out on a tray by Mrs Alexander.

"In fact," said Mr Alexander to the boys, "I've got one or two small jobs that need doing round here and I wondered if you would be interested?"

Freddie looked at Bill but Irving was already responding in an instant.

"Yes, I'd like to help out, Mr Alexander. Will you be able to show me how the

honey is collected?"

"Well, I expected that you all might take turns or help out together, but if you, lad – what's your name?"

"Irving."

"Irving, if you want to help me out, that will be grand."

Freddie spoke in a hushed voice to Bill. "I told you he's going native. First the kippers now the bees."

"Do you want to help out as well?" asked Mr Alexander, hearing the conversation between the two.

"No thanks," said Bill, "it's the sort of thing Irving would be into."

"Well that's splendid, then," said Mr Alexander. "Can he stay with me now?"

Mrs Callaghan smiled. "He's going to miss out on all the scenery, but I don't suppose that he will mind. We come back at about four. I'll pick him up then."

Irving sat at the table with his lemonade as the others started back on their walk. It was one of the few times during a summer vacation when the three had been separated.

Lester Stellings was still in good spirits. He had showered and shaved and made his way down a very broad and grand staircase to the breakfast room which, at nine fifteen, was very full. Lester was rather disappointed; he had hoped to sit alone, perhaps with his newly purchased Daily Telegraph spread across the table, while he tucked into his cooked breakfast. Instead, the manager had asked for his room number and then asked if he minded sharing. Given the crowded room it was very difficult to say that he did. He was led across the room by a young waitress who sat him at a two-seat table. The other person had obviously gone to get, perhaps, some fruit juice or cereal.

Lester ordered a pot of coffee and the full Scottish breakfast. He fleetingly imagined that he might share the table with a woman and where their conversation might lead, but the reverie was rudely interrupted by a hand that pushed his paper flat.

"Move the paper, mate, your spoiling me view."

Before Lester could respond, the part of his paper that was lapping the other side of the table had a large breakfast plate deposited on it.

"I've just gone up for seconds, me. You don't get much in the way of seconds where I've just been."

"Where have you been, then?" said Lester, and then immediately regretted asking. A big face pushed forward in a what-do-you-want-to-know-for attitude. However, the scowl was almost immediately replaced with an attempt at a smile.

"Sorry, mate, I'm a bit jumpy. My name's Deggey Edwards. I've come up from Leicester on business."

"My name's Lester, like the town but spelt with an 's.'"

"What business you here on, Lester? It don't sound like you come from round here."

"It's difficult to explain," said Lester, "but basically I'm up here trying to find some kids."

Deggey eyeballed him hard and suspiciously. "You some sort of nonce?"

"No, no," stammered Lester. "Not like that. I'm trying to trace some missing kids."

Deggey still continued to eyeball him. "You're not a private dick, are you?"

"No, nothing like that, just a friend of the family."

Deggey's attention drifted away for a moment. A short silent pause came between the two of them. Lester looked at Deggey; he seemed to be in a trance. Then suddenly:

"Kids, bleedin' kids, they're nothing but a feckin' nuisance, 'scuse my French. I came up with some yesterday on the train, bloody nuisance they were but they did me a good turn in the end."

"Really," said Lester, beginning to take an interest. But before he could ask more the man had gone distant again and became preoccupied with cutting up the bacon on his plate.

To Lester the man seemed a very rough diamond, not the sort to be taking breakfast in a four-star hotel, but if you were travelling on expenses, he supposed, the hotel saw people from every background.

They both ate in silence for several minutes and then Deggey started to rouse again.

"Do you know where there is a petrol station round here?"

"I'm afraid not; this is my first time here."

"S'pose one can't be far away."

"Why don't you ask at reception?"

"I will, mate, I will, mate," said Deggey, standing up and then he was off and out in a hurry.

What a strange fellow, thought Lester. He was not the sort of person that you would want to come up against in a dark alley-way. It was only as Lester mused as he walked back to his room that it was a odd question that the man had asked about petrol; he had said he had arrived on the train.

Lester went back to his room and started to pack his bag. He was not absolutely sure that he was going to follow the boys, but he wanted more time to think and enjoy himself. He had not had this sort of freedom for years.

All that he had picked up from home was that the boys were staying with a relative somewhere up on the west coast, but not too far from Glasgow. That, he thought, put them a maximum of thirty miles outside Glasgow and he had a list of towns and villages that he was going to pass through to try to track the boys down, along with a few calls to the south to see if he could pick up a more precise location.

Lester was just about ready to leave. He had checked out before breakfast, even having time for a brief, flirtatious conversation with the attractive receptionist. He planned to catch a coach from just outside the hotel that would take him to Dumbarton. From there he would start his search. Lester did a final scour of his room and then, for no particular reason, looked out of the window. He overlooked the main entrance and he could see Deggey striding back to the hotel entrance with a jerrycan in hand.

This all seemed very bizarre. All very well if he wanted to fuel up his car, but who brought petrol into a hotel?

Lester set off down the stairs. Deggey did not pass him and there was no sign of him in reception. Perhaps he had taken the lift? Oh well, what had it to do with him anyway? Lester picked up his bag and made his way towards the main revolving door. At the same time he saw a head come round the door next to the reception desk. It was Deggey and as soon as he recognised Lester, he ducked back behind the door. Lester instinctively knew that something was not right. He moved back towards the door and saw that it was marked "Hotel Staff only, hotel services and basement".

Lester dropped his bag by reception. The staff there were too occupied to notice who was going in and out of the services door, so Lester went on through. A short passageway ran ahead, then turned right and through another door and to steps. Lester could hear footsteps some way ahead and beneath him so he followed cautiously. He went down three flights, always hearing the noise of doors banging ahead of him, though whether it was Deggey or some other hotel worker he could not be sure. Finally he came to the bottom of the stairs and a corridor ran left and right. Left was signposted "Laundry", right signposted "Boiler room".

Lester, on instinct, went right, through another door and was hit by a wall of heat and the distinct smell of fuel oil, but mixed with that the smell of petrol. He could see Deggey ahead of him, the top off the jerrycan, swilling petrol left and right onto the floor.

"What are you doing, you fool? You will set the whole place ablaze."

Deggey looked up, only half surprised now he saw who it was. "Yeh, that's the general idea."

"But there are hundreds of people in the hotel."

"They'll get out, so long as you don't interfere."

Lester realised that for the second time in two days he was going to get into a struggle. He rushed over to Deggey and tried to seize the can from him. However Deggey was far too strong and just threw Lester to the floor.

"Get, out now, while you still can," said Deggey.

Lester looked for a second and then made another dash towards the can.

"You don't learn quick, do you?"

Deggey seized Lester by the arm as he pushed him, and in one move twisted him round so that he was pinned against the wall. With the other hand Deggey took a lighter out of his pocket.

"See this?" Deggey asked, close up to Lester's face, which was screwed against the wall. "Get out now, or 'flick' and the place goes up."

Deggey dropped Lester, who stumbled and then picked himself up and started for the door. He had got on to the stairs and started climbing when he heard a 'whump' and an explosion. Flames shot through the door below him. Lester climbed up to the reception door and shouted "Fire" to the reception staff. As he went back down the stairs again he could hear the alarm bell start in the foyer above him.

Lester went down to the boiler room doors. Flames were lapping on the other side. Lester could not know whether Deggey's plans were suicidal or whether he had planned to lay a fuse and had been interrupted. Lester pushed the door open and could see Deggey lying face down. Lester had once been shown how to give a fireman's lift, but Deggey was a dead weight. Lester dragged him to the stairs and tried to get him upright by putting his backside on the third or fourth step up. Then he was able to tip Deggey forward and across his back and start to lift him up the stairs.

Lester huffed and puffed up the flights and finally reached the reception door. He could now hear the sound of fire engines arriving outside. With a final summons of strength Lester pulled Deggey through the reception door.

The foyer was organised chaos; hotel staff were herding guests outside, the hotel and managers were running left and right yelling commands. Lester and Deggey were noticed and some first-aiders came across.

Several fire-fighters came into the foyer and started to unroll hoses towards the basement.

"It's right at the bottom, in the basement," yelled Lester.

The first-aiders began to ask what had happened. Lester just said that Deggey had been caught in the blast, without adding any further explanation. A stretcher was summoned and Deggey was rolled on to it.

As this was being done, Lester noticed keys which had fallen out of his pocket. Lester palmed these and then made his way out of the foyer with the remainder of the guests.

Two hours later everyone was allowed back in. An ambulance had taken Deggey away. It was said that although a blaze had been started in the basement, it had not reached the fuel oil storage and had been extinguished by the water sprinkler system that was installed in the basement. Apparently the petrol vapour had just caused an explosion and a fireball. The police and fire brigade had started an investigation.

The reception staff had only caught a brief glimpse of Lester and the only person affected seemed to have been Deggey. The hotel was unsure whether Deggey had been involved in setting the blaze or whether, somehow, he was just an innocent victim.

Lester had Deggey's room keys. It was obvious that Deggey had not checked out. Lester wanted to know a bit more about Deggey before he left. He made his way to the room number of the key tag, opened up and went in. There was precious little in the room: a jacket, the rumpled bed and a few scraps of paper, a wallet and some cash on a side table. He looked in the wallet. All of the business cards referred to a Mr Ian Young, a driving licence was in the same name, plus a photo that was obviously not Deggey. Among the scraps of paper was a torn-off corner of a travel warrant issued by Leicester prison. That's more like it, thought Lester. And a torn-off strip from a cigarette packet, with the address 67 Ederline Drive, Helensburgh, written in a childlike hand. That's interesting, thought Lester. Helensburgh was one of his main planned port of calls. He made a mental note of the address and left the room. His bag was still in reception where he had left it. He put Deggey's keys in the key return box and went out of the hotel.

Norman Roberts, the train guard, had not had a good night. He lived in the south but often stayed in Glasgow overnight between journeys north to south. The railways provided a miserly subsistence allowance for overnight stays. It would just about provide bed, breakfast and dinner costs at a low-grade hotel. Norman had found some digs that he regularly used to the west of the city where the prices were low and the grub adequate. This actually left him with a bit of cash over for each journey, which he could add to his meagre wage.

With the thought of the disciplinary hearing on his mind he had hardly touched his supper, spoken to no one in the living room, and had gone to an early bed with a bottle of scotch. He was now deciding that he had drunk too much, before he drifted off into a dream-filled and restless sleep.

That morning he wanted to contact George, to see if he could track down those kids. He took breakfast downstairs, but like the preceding evening his nerves prevented him from eating much.

After breakfast he took a stack of coins to the phone in the hallway and made a call south. It took a few tries to get through to George.

"Hello, is that George Robinson?"

"Yes, it is," crackled the distant voice through a cacophony of background sounds emanating from the mechanical exchange systems that linked them together.

"George, it's Norman Roberts. I saw your kids up to Glasgow on the train yesterday."

"Oh, right, thanks. Any problems?"

"No, not really," lied Norman, "but they left a bag behind in the guard's van and I want to get it forwarded."

"Bloody typical, OK, thanks very much. The address is care of Mr and Mrs Callaghan, 67 Ederline Drive, Helensburgh."

"Thanks, George, I'll get it sent on."

"I'm very grateful. Let me know if it costs and I'll reimburse you."

"No problems, I think I've got that covered. Bye."

"Bye for now."

George Roberts went back to his breakfast. It was only twenty minutes later as he flicked over the pages of the Daily Express that his eyes caught a small item headed "Mayhem on the Glasgow Express".

Police officers met the 0845 London to Glasgow Express after it arrived three hours late in Glasgow yesterday evening. Significant vandalism and a range of criminal activities had taken place during its journey northwards, including a shooting incident at Crewe. Police are continuing to investigate the incidents.

George realised straight away that Norman had not been straight with him and that the boys were almost certainly somehow involved in all of this.

Irving was in his element. For the first time in his life he realised that this was the sort of thing that he wanted to do. He loved these little insects; they seemed so insignificant and yet they were so organised, productive and active. They seemed to put humans to shame. Perhaps they spoke to each other with chemicals like Mr Alexander had said, but they didn't seem to argue and skive like humans did; they just got on with their jobs.

Mr Alexander had got him to assemble three new Langstroth hives and to dismantle and clean two old hives. Irving had really got stuck in to his work because he completed it in half the time that Mr Alexander had expected.

"You've done a good job there, lad. I didn't expect you to be so quick, but you haven't bodged the job."

Irving stood there in the bright sun proudly surveying his handiwork.

"It wasn't difficult, Mr Alexander. If you've got some other jobs like that, I don't mind helping out."

Mr Alexander stood in front of Irving in his overalls and wiped a bead of perspiration from his brow. He took a gold-coloured tin out of his trouser pocket, them a pipe from his shirt pocket and began, painstakingly, to fill it.

"I've not much more work today apart from a bit of clearing up, but you can come up later in the week and help me prepare for the Luss games display."

"What's that, then?" asked Irving.

Mr Alexander took out a box of matches, struck one and held the flame to the bowl of his pipe.

"Every year we have our Highland games down at Luss, beside the Loch. It's more than games, though; it's more like a show and local traders set up stalls. I always set up a bee-keeping stall and sell honey there as well. I usually take along a couple of empty hives and sometimes a glass frame of bees so that the kids can see what goes on in a hive."

"I'd like to help out with that," said Irving.

"Well, it's a hard slog, lots of to-ing and fro-ing from the van to get it loaded and set up, and then the same again at the end of the day."

"I don't mind," said Irving. "I think I will enjoy it."

"Good lad," said Mr Alexander.

Irving had been left some lunch sandwiches. He did the clearing-up that Mr Alexander said that needed doing. Mrs Alexander bought out a pitcher of orange juice and Irving contentedly stretched himself out in the garden, under a shady tree, to await the return of Mrs Callaghan and his brothers.

Marcia was furious. Her mother would not let up. Things had got worse by the minute since her Dad had gone off. She had thought she might have enjoyed herself, just her and her Mum together at home.

The worse of the debris had been cleared from the garden. Scaffolding was erected at the front of the house and a new chimney stack was being constructed. Despite the damage outside, there had been little damage inside. Soot and brick dust had come down most of the chimneys, but this had soon been swept and hoovered up. Cynthia, though, was not happy with this and every nook and cranny had to be wiped down, drawers pulled out, cupboards opened; polish and spray applied to everything.

"But Mum," moaned Marcia, "these drawers haven't been cleaned out in ten years. No soot or dust has got near them."

"That doesn't matter," said Cynthia. "When your father comes back, I want him to come into a house that is spotless. I don't want a single trace of the damage caused by those hoodlum friends of yours."

"They are not friends of mine!" exclaimed Cynthia.

"Friends or not, it's your dealings with them that have brought all this about. This is what comes of living side by side with riff-raff. If we had moved like I have always wanted. you might already be in another school with decent respectable friends of the sort that could be invited to tea. As it is, here we are now a laughing stock. I can't go out, even to the local shops without sideways glances and sniggers."

Cynthia left the room and Marcia became even more depressed. Three days of this, so far. It was driving her mad. She had not set foot outside the house. Not that she really wanted to, but this was the summer holidays. The days were warm and bright outside and here she was trapped in the house. What was more, she was missing her Dad.

There had been a phone call the previous evening. Marcia was sure that it was her Dad on the line, but her Mum had said it was a business call.

When Cynthia was back in the kitchen, Marcia crept to the phone stand and looked at the pad that was kept beneath it. There was one number that seemed to be newly written. She dialled it and a shrill voice announced, "Glasgow Central Hotel".

It must have been Dad calling last night, and that was where he was staying. Marcia crept up to her room, pulled down an old holdall from the top shelf of her wardrobe and started to pile a few clothes into it from each drawer. When she had finished, she rummaged through her bedside locker and picked out her Post Office savings book. She was not going to stay here a moment longer. She had a pretty shrewd idea what her Dad was doing in Scotland. She came out of her bedroom, listened over the banister and could hear clinking noises in the kitchen. Marcia tiptoed down the stairs, silently slipped the latch on the front door and in a moment was up the path and out of the gate.

Irving had dozed off after eating a healthy portion of sandwiches and guzzling most of the pitcher of orange juice. The first he knew of the return of his brothers and Mrs Callaghan were the shouts that intruded on his sleep.

"Wake up, you lazy git," shouted Bill. "I suppose you've been kipping for most of the time that we've been marched around half of Scotland."

Fortunately Mrs Callaghan was out of earshot, talking to Mr Alexander.

Irving roused himself. "In actual fact I've been working most of the day. I've only dozed off the last fifteen minutes or so," he fibbed.

"Well, that's great for you. She's like the Grand Old Duke of York, marching us up and down, look at this, look at that, this is where Mrs Wotshername lives, and Mr Wotshisname used to work here. She never lets up."

"We've got to do something," said Freddie. "Any more of this and I'll go barmy."

"Well, there is one thing that Mr Alexander mentioned," said Irving. "There's supposed to be a Highland games festival at the weekend. Apparently they have stalls all around selling stuff. Perhaps we can get in on the act and set up our own stall."

"Sounds like a good idea," said Bill. "If we can get it past Mrs Callaghan, we might be in with a chance."

Mrs Callaghan came over to the boys with a smile on her face.

"Well done, Irving. Mr Alexander has just been telling me about the splendid job that you have done."

Irving blushed and Freddie and Bill moved around behind Mr Alexander in order to pull faces and mimic Mrs Callaghan's mode of speech.

"You're a credit to your mum. These two ....," she said, turning towards Freddie, who was busy swinging his hips and mouthing "credit to your mum", accompanied by a camp hand gesture.

Freddie froze immediately when he caught Mrs Callaghan's hostile stare.

"These two could learn a lot from you."

They made their farewells to Mr Alexander and made their way back down the hill into Helensburgh.

Later that evening, after they had eaten supper, Mr Callaghan led the boys into his library. The whole room was lined with books from bottom to ceiling. Even their public library at home could not have had so many books.

"In this house," exclaimed Mr Callaghan, "after supper we have time for reflection. I would like you each to choose a book and you can take it into the drawing room to read."

The boys looked around them. They all looked like reference books. Rows and rows of books of the same height with either blue or red spines.

Freddie looked around, anxiously trying to spy out an annual or a book on football. Irving was the first to pipe up.

"Have you got anything on bees?"

Freddie and Bill exchanged glances, but Mr Callaghan was already pointing out a row of encyclopaedias.

"I'm sure you'll find something in there."

Irving could not quite reach the shelf, so Mr Callaghan fetched the book down for him.

Irving went off to look at his book while Bill and Freddie scoured the room for reading matter that might be less than serious. Freddie found a set of map books and started to search for the volume that might hold maps of Scotland, while Bill had come across a set of books to do with battles of the Second World War.

With their books selected, they were guided into the drawing room.

"Half an hour's reading," said Mr Callaghan, "then the radio goes on for the evening concert."

After the first ten minutes of rustling as Bill turned his book round and round in order to get it in the best position for looking at the photographs, Freddie spread out his maps which folded out from the book and then nearly covered him from head to foot. Only Irving seemed immediately engrossed as he poured through the detail of the history of bee-keeping from the ancient Egyptians to the Romans and on to modern times. He was seated in the largest winged armchair and his legs only just poked over the seat cushion as he curled up at the back of the seat.

At seven o'clock Mr Callaghan turned on the old radio set that stood on its own table in the corner. The central dial glowed and a green eye at the top of the set grew from small to large as Mr Callaghan adjusted the tuning. Eventually a BBC voice announced a live relay from The Royal Albert Hall in London. The first part was to be Tchaikovsky's Manfred Symphony.

"This is good, you'll enjoy this," he announced animatedly to the boys. "It's all about man striving against the forces of nature and overcoming his enemies within and without."

The boys exchanged glances with open mouths. There was coughing, more scraping and tuning of musical instruments and then the music began.

They listened intently at first. There were tunes, just, but no singing. They had somehow thought that there would be singing and then after four minutes, when the piece had not come to a finish, there were more glances exchanged by the boys. Irving picked up his book and started to read again. Freddie started to rustle and fidget with his map and Bill dropped his book with a clump as he tried to reposition it on his lap. Mr Callaghan walked to the radio and turned it up a notch.

The music went on. After ten minutes Freddie cracked, "When's this going to finish, Mr Callaghan?"

Mr Callaghan, who seemed to be in a state of trance, eyes closed, angrily responded to Freddie's interruption. "Shush, be quiet while the music is playing. This is the recapitulation of the main theme. There are three more movements to follow." Mr Callaghan returned to his trance state.

"Recap what?" asked Freddie of Bill. "What's a movement?"

With his eyes still shut Mr Callaghan "shushed" again.

Freddie rolled his eyes skywards and began searching for the bit of map that showed the local area. All of the pages seemed to be folded back-to-back and he couldn't find the bit that he wanted.

Something seemed to be happening in the music. Mr Callaghan had raised both his hands and with eyes closed was moving them in sequence to the growing swell of sound. Freddie stifled a snigger; he suddenly realised that the bit of map that he wanted was on the back of the large sheet that now covered him. As the crescendo from the radio grew and grew, he flipped over the sheet and tried to pull it out straight.

Irving had spotted that Mr Callaghan was somewhat distracted. He had read up on 'apiculture' but was certain that more could be found under 'bees'. Now he found he could not reach the shelf again, so he began to take volumes from the lowest shelf and pile them up.

The music still continued loudly and resolutely, and Mr Callaghan's conducting antics were becoming more extreme. He was now mouthing out loud to the music, "ta lah dah, ta ta lah lah dah".

Freddie had tried every way to turn and fold the map page that he wanted, but he could not get the right piece in front of him. He tugged and pulled and the whole sheet began to tear from the book.

Mr Callaghan was now out of his seat, arms raised, eyes still closed. "Ta dah, ta dah, ta daaaah," he sang to final chords, which also coincided with map falling to the floor, completely ripped away from the book. Irving had turned, uncertainly, at the combined noises and as Mr Callaghan at last opened his eyes, the expression of ecstasy fast melting from his face, Irving swayed on the pile of books, made a grab at the shelf in front of him and tumbled with a crash that brought him and a row of books to the floor.

Mr Callaghan turned a very bright shade of red which looked very peculiar against his bottle-green waistcoat.

"You vandal!" he exclaimed at Irving, "Hooligan!"

Mrs Callaghan came rushing into the room at all the commotion. "Whatever is going on?"

"He's ruined my concert," ranted Mr Callaghan, pointing at Bill. "He's ripped my map book," pointing at Freddie, "and he, he ..." stuttered Mr Callaghan, in ex-tremis, pointing at Irving, "he has destroyed my library."

Mr Callaghan was now a very worrying shade of purple, his eyes were red and bulging, and large veins protruded from beneath his collar.

"Steady on," said Bill, "it was only an accident."

"Accident? You've been fidgeting around with that book since the moment the music began."

"Look, I'm sorry about the book," said Bill, "but we didn't ask to hear the concert; we were told to."

"Yeh," said Freddie and there was no singing either and the tunes are rubbish."

Irving joined in. "You said it was about man against nature, but it sounded more like two marching bands having a punch-up. All I could hear was bangs, crashes and shrieking."

"I was waiting for the forces of nature," said Bill. "Where were they? I expected thunderclaps, roaring winds. There was nothing like that."

Mr and Mrs Callaghan listened on in disbelief of what they were hearing. Eventually Mrs Callaghan broke the silence.

Turning to her husband, who was still very red, but now slightly more subdued, she said, "I think we will have to consider some other, more practical activities for the boys. Mr Alexander was very impressed by the work that Irving did today, which goes to show that there are things that will occupy their time positively."

Mr Callaghan looked humbled. "I suppose so. It was too much to expect the boys to be interested in culture."

"Look, I've got a suggestion to make," said Bill.

"We've heard from Mr Irving that there are going to be Highland games and a show at Luss this weekend. If we were allowed to set up a stall, we could sell items and make a donation to the games or whoever organises it."

"Yes," interjected Freddie, "and that's the sort of thing we are good at."

Mr and Mrs Callaghan exchanged glances.

"What sort of things would you be selling?"

"Well, for one," said Bill, "Irving is selling honey and is helping Mr Alexander at his display of bee-keeping, and then we could go around the local shops and see if they've got any old stock that they would be prepared to let us sell."

Mr Callaghan looked dubious. "I can't see many of the Helensburgh traders doing that. They all donate to the games, many of them have stalls there anyway."

"It's worth a try," said Bill. "If we can't get hold of anything, then we'll give up the idea. But give us a chance to let us do what we are good at."

Mr and Mrs Callaghan were surrounded by entreating and pleading stares.

"Well, alright then," said Mr Callaghan. "We will see how your search for items to sell tomorrow goes and then we'll make a final decision about a stall."

The boys' doleful looks immediately changed to smiles of triumph.

"Right then, boys," said Mrs Callaghan, "go out into the back garden, catch the last of the evening's sun and then I'll call you in for a drink."

Once the boys were outside, Mrs Callaghan turned to her husband.

"Don't worry, nothing will come of this. The local traders won't let them have anything because they haven't got licensed stalls. They will spend half a day foraging around and then they will give up the idea."

CHAPTER 4

THE BOYS WERE up and about in good spirits. They tucked their breakfasts down in the knowledge that they would not be traipsing around up hills and down valleys with Mrs C at their lead, but in town doing what they were used to doing on a summer's day.

It was agreed with the Callaghans that they would leave the house at nine o'clock and return by midday with any stock that they had managed to obtain.

As they marched down the hill, Bill gave out the orders for the day.

"Now what we are going to do is to suss out the lay of the land. These traders don't know us. We are going to have to use different tactics to what we use at home. First, we are going to search out the most likely shops and then work from there."

They stopped at a bench that was roughly in the middle of the main row of shops. Bill spoke again.

"If two of us go off up this way," he indicated off to the right and up the slight incline of the road, "and you, Irv, go down on the left-hand side of the street, then we'll meet back here together in fifteen minutes to do the last stretch and then compare notes."

The brothers nodded and set off to their allocated stretch. They took notes of the types of businesses and pressed their noses up to the window glass to see what and who was inside. They each covered their stretches and began to walk back towards the bench.

As they drew close, they could see that the bench was no longer empty but occupied by five kids of about their age, who were lolling and draping themselves over the seat. Freddie, Bill and Irving approached cautiously.

As they came within yards of the bench the biggest lad drew himself to his feet and rounded on Irving.

"Yer new boys around here?" This half question, half statement was delivered in a strong Glaswegian accent and at such a pace that the only word that Irving really picked out was "new".

Irving stared at the gangly lad, who although tall for his age was still a good couple of inches shorter than him.

Irving could see that the other four were sizing the trio up. He looked back at Bill for help in translating. But Bill was offering no help.

"Come again," said Irving. "We speak English, not this bagpipe talk," he said with a grin back at Bill and Freddie, pleased with his attempt at a witticism.

Bill covered his eyes; he could see how this was going to turn out. Fortunately Irving's southern accent and delivery was just as confusing for the Glaswegian lads as their accents were for the trio.

The gangly lad was uncertain of Irving and even more uncertain of what had been said to him, but he had picked up on the English bit.

"If your up from England, then you need to know that this street's ours. Yer no welcome here."

The other four had risen to their feet to stand behind their leader. Irving was looking back for help again. Bill had opened his eyes, again fully expecting to see Irving on the floor.

"What do you want me to do, bruvs?" he asked of Freddie and Bill. "I'll clock this gangly streak and you can take out the others."

Freddie and Bill looked at the other four; the odds were about evens if there was one each but it was going to be a serious scuffle if they tried to take the four. Bill stepped forward.

"Leave it, Irv. We're losers all round if we pick a fight now."

Irving looked despondent. He walked right up to the gangly one and eyeballed him.

"I'm letting you off this time, Scotty dog, but if you pester me and me bruvs again, you'll be playing your pipes through your bum."

The gangly lad drew himself up to meet Irving's face and the other four drew themselves close. They had recognised the tone and attitude of Irving's statement, even though they had only picked up on "Scotty dog" and "bum". They recognised an insult when one was offered them.

Both Freddie's and Bill's hands were over their eyes again, but there was still uncertainty and the babel of dialects had saved the day.

"Let's get off," said Bill, and the trio left the local lads scowling but unsure whether they had triumphed or lost this round.

Freddie, Bill and Irving walked back in the direction they had come from. When they were far enough away, Bill started.

"Irv, you really take the biscuit. You didn't have to start world war three."

Irving took on a hurt and rather confused expression.

"I showed them who is boss, didn't I? They didn't come back with any insults for us."

"Yeh, that's because they didn't understand a word that you said to them. Otherwise we would be laying into each other now and our plans to get supplies for the highland games would be in tatters. As it is we've got to come up with some other strategy. If they see us going into the shops and coming out with stock, there's going to be more aggro."

"We could have had 'em easy though, bruv. You could see that they weren't certain, otherwise they would have jumped us straight off."

"Yeh, alright Irv, we could have had them, but it would not have made our job any easier."

Irving smiled now. "Told you so," he said to the still stunned Freddie.

They mooched away from the town and towards the hills above. Little was said; they were each within their own thoughts. They climbed quite quickly without realising the progress they were making. After twenty minutes they had reached a small road leading into the hills about two miles above the town. Street lamps and road markings had disappeared and only green countryside, rocky outcrops and heather lay in the distance. It had become quite warm now so the trio flopped down on the verge to remove some outer garments.

Marcia was finding getting to Scotland more complicated than she had first expected. She had drawn a total of forty seven pounds from her savings account. When she arrived at Euston station and enquired about ticket prices, she found out that the cost of a ticket was going to be much more than she had been prepared for. Even if she took a risk and assumed that she would meet up with her Dad, and that he would then pay for the return journey, it was still too much. She realised that she had to allow for at least one or two night's bed and breakfast and expenses, for food and for things like bus fares. The sympathetic ticket office worker told her that if she had a student card she could get a discount ticket, otherwise most people of her age travelling north took the over night coach from Victoria which was much cheaper.

An already weary and despondent Marcia took herself off to the underground and headed back towards Victoria. After a short walk along Buckingham Palace Road, she bought her overnight coach ticket leaving at ten thirty that evening. Marcia checked her watch, realised that she had another nine hours before the coach left and so bought a cheap sandwich, a cup of coffee and curled up on a bench with a book to wait.

For almost ten years Hamish McCann and Julie Fennel had passed each other in their respective vans on the long high roads between Helensburgh and Luss, Garelochhead and Faslane, serving the small village communities and individual homes and farms that lay between them. Julie drove the Loch Lomondside library bus and Hamish the Helensburgh mobile shop and provisions van. Both of them also acted as an unofficial bus service and often dropped locals off between villages and towns, It was often on the lonely Glen Fruin Road, near Auchenvennel, across the hills above Faslane, that they would pass again at lunchtime and give each other a friendly wave. Frequently one of them would have to give way to the other's vehicle and as they passed alongside each other, they would spend a few minutes passing the time of day and repeating the local gossip.

It took nearly five years of this, winter, autumn, spring and summer before they realised that they were both single, enjoyed each other's company and were in a position to make more of their relationship.

The problem was that they lived some distance from each other and neither of them had their own transport. The only way forward for their courtship was to extend the time of their meetings near Auchenvennel. If either of them carried a passenger, they did not stop, merely waved and flashed headlights. Depending on the passenger a kiss might surreptitiously be blown or mock grimace made to indicate the burden imposed by the passenger on their relationship.

On the occasions when they were both free of passengers their relationship had blossomed. From lunch taken together in one of their vans, ended with a fond embrace and parting kiss, the time taken consuming food had considerably diminished in favour of mutual appreciation, and the now, nearly hour-long reunion times were spent cuddling and rolling on the floors of their respective vans. Julie's was preferred as the shelves could be moved to give them a considerable amount of floor space, and between the L–Rs and S–Zs of modern fiction they wrote their own chapter of passion. The only drawback to her van was that it was lower down and if, as happened on rare occasions, a walker should pass the van, it was possible that they might peer in.

Hamish's van was much more restricted, piled up as it normally was with stock. However, it did leave a central strip available to the two of them. In the late autumn, winter and early spring months Hamish's van was much warmer and as the sun started to lay low in the sky, even in the early afternoon, Hamish and Julie could lay locked in embrace in the quiet twilight amidst the scents of apples, pears, cheeses, polishes and cleaning fluids.

Once stripped to their waists in the warm afternoon sun, Freddie, Bill and Irving made their way along the road into the hills. Each of them muttered in turn about what they were going to do and how they should have perhaps stayed and confronted the Glasgow boys. After about half an hour or more or climbing they reached an oval area beside the road that was obviously used as a collecting point for local refuse. The boys casually looked through the piles of debris, which mostly consisted of old wooden furniture and mattresses and sofas, both with springs and plumes of filling spilling out in various places. Bill slumped himself down in an old armchair, Irving did likewise on a tired and buckled sofa. Freddie alone carried on rummaging and scavenging amongst the piles. Eventually he hauled out an old radio set which he held up triumphantly.

"And what exactly are you going to do with that?" demanded Bill.

Freddie looked it over and placed it on a nearby rock and said, "Wait and see."

He disappeared off behind some rocks while Bill and Irving speculated about what he was going to do. Freddie reappeared with several fist-sized rocks clutched to his chest, dropped all but one to the floor and aimed that at the radio case.

"I knew it," shouted Irving at Bill.

Bill and Irving were immediately out of their seats and round by the rocks gathering their own ammunition.

A vicious onslaught began which only paused for seconds as the remains of the radio case was replaced on the rock so that it could receive further shots. Wood cracked and splintered, glass valves shattered and exploded and the radio set was quickly reduced to tiny pieces. The boys anger had been vented and Freddie picked among the remains to take out a couple of magnets which he shoved deep into his pocket for future entertainment.

The boys were up again and walking on with a new sense of purpose. They rounded a bend in the road to see two large vans parked close to each other on a long grassy verge. They stopped still.

"What's going on here, then?" asked Irving of the other two.

Although they were still one hundred yards away, they could see that the drivers' seats seemed to be empty.

"Don't know," said Bill, "but we're going to find out. Quietly does it."

They crept up to the first of the vans which was the library van. Everything was completely silent. All they could hear was the odd twitter from a bird high overhead.

"There must be somebody about," whispered Bill. "Unless they've gone off for a picnic. Here you are, Irv. See if you can look over the window."

Bill give Irving a leg up so that he could look in through the side window. He scanned inside for a bit then dropped down to his brothers.

"There's a couple at it on the floor," he sniggered.

"What do you mean, 'at it'?" asked Freddie dumbly.

"You know what I mean, 'at it', 'doing the business.'"

Realisation dawned on Freddie's face, leaving him with reddening cheeks.

"Well let's leave them to it while we case the other van."

The walked the few yards to the other vehicle, slowly recognising the meaning of script on the side.

"Bingo," said Irving excitedly.

"Aladdin's cave," muttered Bill.

"Question is," said Freddie, "how are we going to lay our hands on all these goodies without getting caught?"

The three of them examined the situation before them with the eyes of experts. Bill turned to the other two.

"We'll let off the handbrake and push it out of sight before we see if we can unload any stock."

"Yeh," said Freddie, "but even so, if we get the stock off out of sight, how are we going to get it back home? We're miles away."

"Let's move it first," said Bill. "Then we'll sort it out from there."

Irving tried the driver's door which was open and the keys were still in the ignition. He let off the handbrake and they pushed the van quietly across the grass verge. Once they were back on the road, the van moved more swiftly and they rolled it on round the corner and out of view.

"What are we going to do now?" asked Freddie. "We can't drive the van back, we'll get stopped in no time."

"No," responded Bill, "I've thought this through. Irv, you can drive, can't you?"

"I've driven a car, but nothing as big as this," responded Irving.

"Doesn't matter, we're only driving a little way up the road until we find some old farm buildings or somewhere we can hide the van. Then we'll take some stock off and hide it somewhere else and come back for it later. If they find the van, then they'll assume that the stock is long gone."

"Sounds brilliant," said Freddie, "but haven't we forgotten something? We don't normally rob a whole shop. Most of the stuff is given to us, we just add a little extra to it."

"I know what you mean," said Bill. "We don't want to become known as hardened criminals. My idea was that we can sell some of this stuff at the Highland games and if anything is left, we'll give it back plus a share in the profits. That way the owner will have the money to buy new stock and nobody loses out apart from the inconvenience that we're causing. On the other hand the van driver is going to have some pretty hard explaining to do about what he was doing away from his van."

Freddie and Irving grinned.

"Let's go for it then, bruvs," said Irving.

Irving turned the engine over and it sprang to life and slowly lolloped down the road for a mile or two until they came to two small turnings off to the left.

"Just drive up there a bit," Bill said to Irving.

After about twenty yards up one of the tracks Bill indicated to stop. He jumped out and ran back behind the van and then got back in.

"I thought so," he said to the other two. "We've left tracks where we've turned off. We'll reverse and go down the other track as well and do the same again somewhere else. That should keep them guessing."

About a mile further on they turned down another track and shortly afterwards saw another leading towards a big tin-roofed shed which had probably been used for keeping livestock in. They pulled the van around behind it so that it was completely invisible from the road above it.

"This will do," said Bill. "If we get some stock unloaded from the back we can hide it down there." He pointed to a smaller shed downhill, some fifty yards away.

The boys set to, unloading the van, not taking everything, but something of most. After twenty minutes they had taken most of what they wanted. Irving kept on going back for more.

"Leave it out," said Freddie. "We've got more than enough. We want to set up a stall not a bloody warehouse."

Irving reluctantly put down most of what he was carrying but came out with three little blue bottles.

"What are they, then?" asked Freddie.

"It's for blowing bubbles."

"What on earth do you want that for?" demanded Freddie.

"You never know," retorted Irving.

"No, I don't suppose I ever will," said Freddie, shaking his head in despair.

They covered up their haul with straw, made sure there was no sign of fresh tracks from the shed to the tin barn and started walking back up the road. Almost two hours had passed since they had taken the van. They started the slow trudge back towards Helensburgh.

After about half an hour of walking they heard the noise of an engine coming towards them.

"Should we hide?" asked Freddie.

"No, it's too late," said Bill. "It's almost on top of us, we'll be seen."

The big blue front of the library van raced towards them. Bill spoke quickly to his two brothers.

"This is going to take some good acting."

The boys looked up. The van pulled to a sharp halt in front of them. A very red-faced Hamish McCann was at the wheel and Julie beside him. Hamish wound down the windows and addressed the boys.

"Where have you lads just come from?"

"We've been up in the hills," said Bill.

"All day long?"

"Yes, we're exploring the area."

"You haven't seen a green provisions van on the road or parked somewhere as you've come down?"

The boys looked from one to another, a picture of innocence.

"No, no green van," said Freddie. "Have you lost one then?" he added.

Hamish looked as if he might explode but Julie quickly interrupted.

"They're only kids; there's no reason why they should have known about it."

"They're the only people we've come across today and if they have been up above, they might have spotted something."

"Are you sure you've seen nothing?"

"We saw some sheep," said Freddie in a way that sounded as if it might help.

"No, no," said Hamish, "I'm still talking about a green van."

"Is it your van then that's gone missing?" asked Irving.

"My employer's van, with a month's supply of provisions in it. Someone took it while I was on lunch break."

"Taking a lie down, were you?" asked Irving, with the vaguest of winks.

Hamish went redder again and started to look at Irving in a strange way. Bill could hardly bear to think what Irving would come out with next.

"If any of you know about this, you should say now; the police will be involved."

"Like we said, we've been of up in the hills. We've seen no one else all day, until you turned up," said Bill.

Hamish and Julie exchanged glances.

"Where do you boys come from? You don't look like locals," asked Julie.

"We're staying with an aunt in Helensburgh. Any chance of a lift back there now?"

Hamish looked exasperated. "We haven't got time for that now; we've got to trace the van."

"It won't do any harm," said Julie. "We might as well head back that way now. There might have been a report or a sighting."

"Oh well," said Hamish reluctantly, "get on board then."

The three boys, with grins to each other, climbed on via the side door and the van pulled off. It was about a twenty-minute drive down into the town and Hamish and Julie were silent throughout. The van pulled up in the town centre and the boys got up to get off.

"Just one thing that I've thought of," said Freddie. "There were some Glasgow boys we passed on the way up this morning."

"Oh yes," said Hamish, immediately interested.

"Yeh, they were messing around on the road out of town."

"Did they say where they were going?"

"No, but they had a cart with them."

"Cart, what sort of cart?"

"It was a trailer thing, weren't it Bill? Like they have on the back of cars, with two wheels. Don't know what they were doing with that."

Hamish nodded at Julie. "That's more like it. I think we know the kids you're talking about. Thanks then, bye."

"Bye," the boys echoed.

They were fifty yards up the road and out of earshot before Irving slapped both of his brothers on their backs.

"Two birds with one stone. Brilliant that was, Freddie."

Bill turned to the two of them. "You're both getting worse by the day. The general idea is to get out of these scrapes by acting innocent, not setting others up for our crimes. Now the van driver's going to go straight to the police. The Glasgow boys are going to get nicked and just who's going to be in the firing line when they realise that they've been set up?"

"Yes, but by that time we'll have the stock and the driver and the police will have been on a wild goose chase, and the Glasgow boys will have been locked up," said Irving.

"Yes, and they'll come out of the nick with one thought on their minds: finding us and getting their own back."

"I'm sure we can cope with that," said Irving.

"Let's hope so. Meantimes we've got to get our stock. We're going to need transport and a night-time outing."

"The only person we've seen with a van is that Mr Alexander."

"Well, that's it," said Bill. "We'll need to pay him a visit after dark."

Irving looked upset. "But you can't take his van; he's supposed to be helping us out."

"Needs must," said Bill.

The three of them were approaching their aunt's home. It was early evening now and they were supposed to have been back by lunchtime. Before they could reach the front door, it was whipped opened and Mrs Callaghan came out.

"Where ever have you been? We've looked all over town. Nobody had seen you and you were supposed to be back here for lunch."

"Sorry," said Bill, "but we had a misunderstanding with some local lads and had to get out of the way."

Mr Callaghan poked his nose inquisitively through the doorway. He was dressed in his normal bottle-green waistcoat.

"You didn't manage to get anything for your stall then?" he asked hopefully with a glance to his wife.

"Oh yes," said Freddie, "we got plenty, but we had to hide it away as the local gang was after it."

"Oh dear," said Mr Callaghan.

"Yeh," said Bill, "we're going to pick it all up tomorrow morning for the games."

"Well, you better come on in now and get some tea, you must be famished, being out all day."

The boys took off their holdalls, jackets and boots and were lead in the dining room where it seemed that sandwiches and cakes were in piles that went all the way up to the ceiling. The boys did not have to be asked twice. They were all hungry and they lay siege to the food, gulping down glasses of lemonade between every few mouthfuls. Freddie and Bill were exhausted after several helpings. It was only Irving who ploughed on with a seemingly inexhaustible appetite.

Eventually Mr and Mrs Callaghan, who had evidently already eaten, came back into the room. "We thought we would let you play in the garden again for a bit, and then you can get an early night's sleep."

"That sounds like a good idea," said Bill. "I'm feeling tired already."

The boys went out to the garden. As soon as they were far enough from the house, Bill turned to his two brothers and said, "We've got two immediate problems to overcome. First, we've got to get out tonight. Second, we've got to get hold of Alexander's van. The rest is easy – we get the stock from the van and bring it back here."

"I still don't like the idea of taking Alexander's van. He's helped us out," said Irving.

"Helped you out, you mean," said Freddie.

"Alright, I know it's me," said Irving, "but it can benefit us all."

"How do you reckon that?" asked Freddie.

"Well, I'm supposed to be helping Alexander out during the games. I might be able to persuade him to let us set up shop next to him; then we would be semi-legit."

"It's an idea," said Bill. "Anyway our toughest job could be getting out of here. Any ideas?"

"We could spike their evening drink," said Freddie.

"I don't know," said Bill. "I've seen Mr Callaghan with an evening tipple but not Mrs C."

"We could lock them in their room," said Freddie. "That's what they done to us."

"Too risky," said Bill. "If one of them gets up, they will know we are up to something and the whole thing could unravel. I think one of us has to get out first, say half an hour ahead of the others. Then if the Callaghans check, we can make sure it looks as though we're all here."

"Well, in that case," said Irving, "it had better be me that volunteers to get Alexander's van. I can get it started, one way or another, and fetch it down here to pick up you two."

"OK," said Bill, "you'll make the first move at twelve thirty, and we will be outside at one o'clock. Agreed?"

Freddie and Irving nodded.

They were in bed shortly after nine thirty after another drink and biscuits. The evening light lingered late in the northern hemisphere, and it seemed an age before it was completely dark and they heard the Callaghans go up to their room. Another hour passed with the boys dozing and waking.

At twelve thirty by the bedroom clock, Irving changed back into his clothes and picked up his shoes, which he carried with him. Both Freddie and Bill were at the door of their rooms listening as he descended the stairs. There was barely a creak. But they did hear the faintest click of the front door. He would have jumped the front gate.

Freddie went into his room and put the two pillows on Irving's side.

The two lads waited. Nothing for twenty minutes and then a padding across the landing and Bill's door was pushed ajar, just a few inches. Bill feigned the quiet sighs of sleep and the padded steps returned from where they came.

Ten minutes later both boys were down the stairs and out of the door in seconds, leaving it on the latch.

"I hope that's the only check they do tonight," said Bill, "or we're for it."

Bill and Freddie walked up the hill. It was quiet; no cars, no people, just a quiet residential street. They climbed the hill quickly and then could see a car with sidelights coming over the hill. It approached slowly and suddenly pulled across the road to their side.

"Get in," whispered Irving.

The side door was flung open and Bill and Freddie climbed aboard. The car did a U-turn and went off back up the hill.

"It's lucky they are so trusting round here," said Irving. "The keys were in the ignition and the car was even pointing in the right direction. No one heard a thing."

They headed quickly to the edge of town. Not one car passed in either direction and then they were up towards the hills on the road over towards Faslane. Irving put on the main beam now and it was not too long before they spotted the recess where they had destroyed the old radio. A little further on was the wide verge where the vans had been parked and then they were looking for the turnings off where they had first tried to find a hiding spot for the van. They counted a couple of tracks on the right.

"By my reckoning," said Bill, "there should be one more turning on the left and then the track we went down on the right."

They reached the turning, rose at first and then travelled downhill, but there was no sign of the big tin-roofed building.

"Bugger," said Bill. "We've got it wrong. Stop the car, Irv."

Irving pulled to a stop and switched off the engine.

"Kill the lights," said Bill. The lights went out and they were plunged into the blackest of black nights.

"Come on, get on out," said Bill. They groped for the door handles and collided with one another as they climbed out into the cool night air.

"What's the point of this?" said Freddie. "I can't even see my hand in front of my nose."

"Me neither," complained Irving.

"Give it five minutes," said Bill. "Your eyes will soon adjust."

They waited and gradually the outline of the hills around them grew clear and what had been a black veil above them slowly filled with a myriad stars.

"It's bloody marvellous," said Freddie. "You can see like it's day."

Freddie and Irving looked up into the sky and the large stars of the constellations seemed to grow bigger and brighter. They could see the flow of the Milky Way and the fields of stars beyond stars. They stood transfixed, looking into the deepness of the universe, all thoughts of the present gone.

"Look," said Freddie, "that's the constellation of Hercules, and that's Cygnus. We did that in school."

Freddie and Irving laid down on the soft heather to get a greater panorama of the skies.

"A shooting star!" exclaimed Irving.

"Where?"

"For goodness sake, give over you two," said Bill. "We're trying to find a barn not bleedin' Pluto."

Freddie and Irving snapped out of their reverie. Irving scanned around.

"There's no sign of any building here. I reckon we were further down and that we missed this track first time over."

"Could be," said Bill, " but I don't see how we missed it in the daylight. Everything looks different now."

They turned back towards the van and were just about to climb in.

"Hang on," said Freddie. He had spotted what Irving had just caught a glimpse of. A slight brightening on the horizon, and then again.

"Car lights," said Bill, "coming on the main road."

They waited, still, as the lights drew closer. They would not be seen from where they were provided the car didn't turn down the track.

The car moved at a slow speed past the track end.

"Police car," said Freddie.

"Yeh," said Bill. "I think that they think they're on to something. They know the van and provisions are up here somewhere and they are waiting for it to be moved. We're going to have to be extra cautious."

They waited until all sign of the lights of the car had disappeared and then started the van, side lights on only. They crept on for half a mile until they found another turning.

"What do you think of this one?" said Bill to the other two.

"Could be," said Freddie hesitantly, "but I thought our track was narrower."

"Go for it, Irv," said Bill.

They swung off and went downhill. After a few seconds they saw the outline of the tin-roofed building ahead. Irving cut the engine and lights and they coasted down to it.

They walked around behind it and could see the grocer's van hidden away. They were just about to walk down towards the shed when they each heard the thud of a heavy carton being dropped.

"The Old Bill have got to it first," said Freddie in despair.

"I don't think so," said Bill. "Their lights went on way past this point."

"What then?" asked Irving.

The three crept towards the hut, making sure that they made no sound and were out of sight. They got to the corner of the hut and went down on the ground.

Irving pushed his head forward to look. He withdrew it quickly and in urgent, hushed tones said, "It's them Scotty boys, they're loading their own van."

Bill and Freddie pushed their heads forward. There was a torch lying on the ground sending a little light towards the back of a dark van, and the Glasgow lads were busy putting the stock that had been stashed in the van.

Freddie, Bill and Irving turned back to each other.

"How did they get to find out about this?" said Freddie. "I thought they would have been locked up by now."

"My guess," said Bill, "is that the police questioned them, they denied it and then worked out that it was probably us that had done it. Since they had been blamed, they came to find our loot."

"That makes sense," said Irving. "What are we going to do now? Take them on? I'm up for it!"

"No," said Bill. "We're going to stitch them again." He signed to follow him and the three went back to the tin barn.

"We can't move the van back up to the road and if we start it they will hear."

Bill went into the grocer's van and handed down a couple of boxes that remained on the van.

"Fred, you give me a hand with these and Irving, you push our van round the back of the barn, out of sight."

Freddie and Bill took the boxes up to the road and stacked them at the beginning of the track but in clear view from the road. Irving came up to join them.

"What now?"

"Well, if I'm right, that police car's going to be back this way soon."

"If you're wrong," said Freddie, "then we've lost our stock and the Scotty boys have got one over on us. It's not going to take them much longer to load up."

They waited about four agonising minutes that seemed like hours before car lights appeared on the horizon.

"I just hope it's them," said Bill.

"First time you've wanted the police to be on our case," commented Freddie. "Knowing how sharp they normally are, they're going to sail straight past."

The light drew closer and the lads crept out of sight. Once the car was within a few hundred yards they could see it was the police car, travelling slowly again. The headlights swayed towards their turning. The beams travelled over the cartons but the car went on past.

"What the ..." said Irving. "Thick or what?"

In exasperation Irving picked up a stone and before Bill or Freddie could stop him, he had stepped out behind the car and sent the stone skimming towards it.

Clunk – it hit soundly on the metal of the boot. Brakes were slammed on and two burly figures emerged from the car. They quickly switched on torch lights. Irving had now been wrestled to the ground by his brothers. He was so agitated that he was still trying to shout out.

"Whaa ..."

Bill shoved his whole hand into Irving's mouth and, with Freddie, dragged him into a bush.

The burly policemen approached with their torches.

"Wa did those boxes come from? I did na see them just now."

The three lads could almost hear the cogs turning in their heads.

Fortunately the rest was done by the Glasgow boys, who now roared up the track in their van, knocking the cartons flying as they took the corner and sending the policemen spinning onto the verge. The police gathered their senses, ran back to their car and set off after the Glasgow boys.

Irving was back, speaking again.

"What are we going to do now? We've lost our stock."

"We've lost that stock, but we can have second best. What's left on the grocers van, plus those cartons," he said, pointing at the contents which were scattered across the road.

"The police will soon catch up with the Glasgow boys, given their weight plus what's on their van, and we're in the clear now. All we have to do now is to get back safely with our provisions. If we take the road on to Faslane, we can get into Helensburgh on the main road, which means we don't have to pass the Glasgow boys."

"What, no punch-up?" bewailed Irving.

Bill and Freddie just gave him a sideways glance.

The boys were back at the Callaghans' at three, the door still on the latch as they had left it. Mr Alexander's van was back where it had been taken from and the provisions safely cached in a garage they had spotted near to Mr Alexander's house.

Clothes off, back into bed, the three slept the sleep of innocents until after dawn.

CHAPTER 5

THERE HAD BEEN Highland games at Luss for centuries. Modern games had taken place there since 1875. In olden days the games consisted largely of trials of strength and stamina that temporarily settled rivalries between clans. Cabers were tossed, hammers thrown, stanes were put, weights lifted and teams strained their might in tugs of war. In the late nineteenth century the games was the annual event to which all came. Best clothes were donned, the children were groomed, and the horse and carts brought people to the games from all localities.

As the twentieth century progressed, the games started to attract visitors: forgotten clan members anxious to retrace and re-establish their roots and the increasing flow of tourists from within the UK and abroad. Commercial sideshows attached themselves to the central sporting events, which themselves now included track events and displays of Scottish dancing and piping.

By the 1960s all forms of Scottish country life were on display at the games: shooting, hunting, dog breeding, fishing, wildlife, Scottish cuisine. Whatever it was, it was to be found somewhere in the arena.

The talk of this year's games was of the Canadian and Japanese competitors for tossing the caber. Archie McCulloch, 24-stone, red of beard, arrived in the locality with his entourage in late July and paraded himself around town in his Cadillac and bright yellow jacket and blue breeches. His entourage consisted of about fifteen cheerleader girls who were supposed to lend a New World aspect to the traditional event, but who became notorious locally by getting drunk, and for their screaming and shrieking.

Archie claimed descent from a local clan from which an ancestor had departed for the Canadian Rockies in the early 1800s. Archie's family had done well, or so he told anyone willing to listen, in the logging business, and he was back to show off his wealth and prowess in the physical feats of his ancestors.

Yukio Mukikeendo claimed he was the descendant of a nineteenth-century traveller, Robbie McKeen, who had taken malt whiskey to the Japanese people. His boat had been shipwrecked near Sapporo on the island of Hokkaido in 1824. Robbie had spent three days in the sea and was finally washed ashore during a storm. He hammered on the door of the nearest house and, because of his condition and experience, was taken for a spectre of the sea. All the local fishing families came to revere him and would consult him before taking their boats to the sea in stormy weather.

As husbands perished, Robbie would go to their widow with bottles of malt, which continued to be washed ashore, to console them. Before he died in 1839 from liver failure, he had fathered twenty-four sons and thirty-two daughters among the small fishing community.

Yukio was small of stature but immensely strong, and a contender for many of the heavy events. Before the games he would impress the locals in the inns of Luss by cracking open three walnuts on a table with one blow of his forehead.

Freddie, Bill and Irving were totally ignorant of these traditions. They saw the event as merely a chance to sell on their ill-gotten gains, and hopefully to avoid the Glasgow boys who would almost certainly be out looking for them.

They had partaken of the normal over-large breakfast. The Callaghans were to be at the games, but seemed to have resigned themselves to the fact that Irving would be helping Mr Alexander and that the other two boys would be selling some of their own items nearby.

The lads had decided that they would all help load up Mr Alexander's van in the hope that they would be able to put their own provisions aboard. They were not really sure how they could get everything on the van in one go. They planned that once Mr Alexander became preoccupied with his display, they might be able to get more of their own stock down to the stall.

Mr and Mrs Callaghan made sure that the boys looked reasonably smart and arranged to meet them at the games at about ten forty five for the opening. The boys, happy to be free again, set off up towards Mr Alexander's house. They turned into his back gate to find Mr Alexander unloading boxes from his garage.

"Here you are at last," he said to the boys. "I was hoping that you would be up here earlier; there's a lot to do."

"What do you need help with. Then?" asked Irving.

"Well, if you could start loading up the van with these boxes of honey, then I can sort out the glass frame that we are taking, and the made-up hives."

"We've got one or two things that we want to take to the games ourselves," said Bill. "We're hoping that we might be able to set up our own side stall."

Mr Alexander paused. "I don't know about that. There are strict rules on who can set up shop there."

"I know," said Bill, "but the Callaghans seem think it is OK."

"I'll be checking," said Mr Alexander.

The boys were left to start loading the boxes of jars into the van. As soon as Mr Alexander had disappeared, Bill sent Freddie and Irving down to the garage to get the first of their provisions. They managed to get quite a lot of it squeezed into the back of the van with the boxes of honey hiding it.

When Mr Alexander returned, he expressed some surprise that the boxes had taken up so much space, but he did not question further and so they set off with their first load to the games arena.

The entrance to the games field was chaotic. People were already arriving and goods vans and cars were trying to pass each other to get in and out. Marshals sported armbands and they were trying to provide a bit of order amidst the chaos. Mr Alexander queued for a few minutes and then his van and the boys went through and drove around the edge to an area at some distance, but opposite, the main stand. Mr Alexander had already set up his stall inside a small tent that had been erected for most of the stallholders in case of bad weather. Mr Alexander jumped out and went off in search of an official, giving the boys instructions to unload the van.

This was the freedom that the three wanted. Bill and Freddie left Irving with the boxes and some beehive equipment while they went off in search of some trestle tables. They soon found some extras at a catering stall and left Mr Alexander's name as guarantee. From then on it was plain sailing. Freddie and Bill were setting up stall like in the old days, and Irving was keeping Mr Alexander occupied.

After a while Mr Alexander set off back with Irving to get the rest of the bee-keeping display and Freddie and Bill were putting the finishing touches to their stall. Bill turned to Freddie and said, "As soon as we're finished here, we'll take a look around. Suss out the lie of the land and see who our competitors are."

Freddie nodded in agreement. They placed a few more neatly written labels on items and then set off round the field.

Marcia had had a very long and tedious journey up to Scotland. She had variously read and slept on her bench for hours. As it drew close to the time of the coach's departure, she walked round to the bay from which the coach was to leave, only to be horrified at the length and make-up of the queue that was already waiting. For some reason she had imagined that she might be one of a few overnight passengers.

A broad column of student types, each laden down it seemed with several bags, rucksacks and carriers, stretched away from the bay and along the adjacent wall. They all seemed to have long hair and beards. Even the few girls that she could make out looked distinctly odd.

Once she finally came to board, she was forced to sit alongside a very smelly individual who reeked of tobacco, alcohol and some other heavy scent that she could not put a name to. He made a grunt and muttered "Hi man" as she squeezed alongside him, but that was his sole communication during a ten-hour journey. He resolutely refused to move up the seat and Marcia was left to perch on the edge.

The coach crawled on in the early hours of the morning towards its Scottish destination, taking frequent stops at service stations along the route. Marcia slept not a wink, although she managed to angle herself in her seat so that it became vaguely comfortable. She imagined meeting up with her father in Glasgow and the thought of his friendly smile and big arms around her were her only consolation during the journey.

The coach finally squealed to a halt within the fume-filled, grubby halls of the Glasgow coach station. Marcia was out and asking directions to the station hotel in no time at all. She arrived there within fifteen minutes and asked the receptionists for the number of her fathers' room.

"Mr Stellings, Mr Stellings. Oh here it is. Oh no, he checked out two days ago."

"Oh no," echoed Marcia. "Did he leave a forwarding address?" She felt a sinking feeling within, her feet felt leaden and her voice had become hoarse.

"No, I'm afraid, nothing on the card. Nothing at all."

"Would anyone know?" she asked in desperation.

"I'll just check out back; there might have been someone out back on duty when he checked out."

A short, attractive, red-headed girl came out. "Mr Stellings, is he your father?"

"Yes," replied Marcia hopefully.

"Yes, well, I'm sure it was Mr Stellings, and there does seem to be a resemblance. He mentioned he was travelling along through coast towns towards Helensburgh."

"And that was two days ago," said Marcia. "He must already be there by now."

"If you manage to meet up with your Dad, could you ask him to contact the Manager here?"

"Why's that?" asked Marcia, surprised.

"We think it was your Dad that did a very useful service to the hotel. We would like to hear from him."

Marcia thanked the receptionist and said that she would pass the message on, but she could not think what sort of service her father could have provided the hotel.

Marcia caught the bus towards Dumbarton at the same stop that her father had departed from. She was a little easier now that she had a destination to head towards, but still conscious that she was very low on funds if she had to stop overnight.

The Luss Highland games began with the entry march of the Chief of the Clan onto the games field, preceded by a full highland marching band, dancers and a parade of competitors. It was only Archie McCulloch and his cheerleaders and the squat Yukio Mukikeendo who looked out of place and the noises from the stand

as they passed by indicated that the public reaction towards them had cooled considerably.

Before the games themselves commenced, a secondary entertainment, the Dumbartonshire Miniature Pipers, came onto the field. In number this was a full piping band, but it was made up of children dressed as adults with fake beards and moustaches. As the marching parade turned and the band passed through its own ranks, the pipers linked arms and performed a series of jigs while still continuing to play. The drummers did likewise, twirling their drumsticks as they turned together. The audience seemed to love them and gave rapturous applause.

"Pathetic really," said Freddie, as he looked on with his brothers. "Why bother to get kids dressed up like that if you've got the real thing?"

"Scottish tradition, I suppose," said Irving.

"Still pathetic, I say," said Freddie. "I'm sure that it could be improved."

The boys made their way back towards their stall. They had looked around. There were many eateries, whisky-tasting stalls, providers of game and other highland delicacies, but few were selling many basic provisions.

"We should make a fortune at our prices," said Bill.

They set to work. Irving was selling jars of honey at a tremendous rate and eagerly showing visitors the glass frame, a cross-section of a hive with honeycomb, queen and worker bees going about their tasks.

Every now and again everyone would turn as a roar came from the heavy events or the track.

Mr Alexander came and went. Mostly he left Irving to get on with it. He lit his pipe and chatted by the tent flap to the locals, most of whom he knew by first name. Sometimes he wandered off to chat at another stall or to take a closer look at the field events.

Some two hours had passed since the opening. Irving was bending down, opening up yet another carton to put new jars on display. Suddenly he was aware that it had gone darker. The flaps of the tent had been undone and pulled across so that the front was now closed. He looked up. He was surrounded by the Glasgow boys.

"Got yer on yer own now, yer long streak," said the tallest of their group. "What yer doin' here sellin' honey and shewin' off bees?"

Irving said nothing. He just nonchalantly picked up a couple more jars of honey and added them to the display.

The Glasgow lad had moved his head to one side to nod at his mates. As he turned again, Irving stepped back and taking advantage of his height and the boy's head angled towards him, head-butted him hard. The boy flew backwards through the piled honey jars and crashed onto the floor on the base of the display glass, which fell to the ground.

At the sound of this, Bill and Freddie came running from next door and taking in the scene, laid in to the remaining four of the gang. The lad on the floor was staying where he was and with Irving it was three on four. However it was hard work; the Glasgow lads were good scrappers and no sooner as one was laid on the floor than another was back up at them. The tent's contents were devastated, the bee frame broken open and the small swarm had escaped.

The fighting continued. At one moment Irving had tripped and the Glasgow lads were getting the better of them. At this point the tent flap opened again and a dark figure stood in the entrance.

"Having bother, boys?" came the deep, gruff question. It was Torchy. "I told yer I would return your favour."

He picked up a couple of the Glasgow lads as if they were rag dolls and swung them together so that their heads cracked. Even Irving winced. The remaining two saw their comrades' fate and ran.

Torchy was just helping the lads to their feet when Mr Alexander came through the flap. He saw the carnage.

"Good God! What has happened here?"

"It's not the boys' fault," said Torchy. "They were set upon by a Glasgow gang."

"Everything's wrecked," said Mr Alexander. "I'm going to have to call the police."

He started to pick up small bits of the glass frame.

At the mention of the word "police", Torchy was lost from sight.

The caber-tossing event was reaching a climax. Given the number of competitors, heats had been held. Caber-tossing performance is awarded points not just for the distance thrown but for style and how the caber is balanced and turned within the throwing circle.

Five contestants remained for the finals. Three locals plus Archie and Yukio. The locals were getting heartily fed up with the antics of the newcomers. They wanted one of the local clansmen to win. Every time Archie threw, there was this ridiculous charade of cheerleaders shouting and jumping behind him, and even Archie himself had to do an additional pirouette with the caber before it was thrown. As some of the locals were now commenting, this was a caber-tossing event, not country dancing. Archie would be better off across the field with the pipers.

Even more frustrating was the antics of Yukio. Even though he wore a kilt, for every throw he would approach the caber in a traditional Japanese robe and perform some sort of chanting before it, which involved at least a dozen separate bows. There was no doubt about it, though; he was a good thrower.

Two locals had thrown in the finals. It was now Archie's turn. The cheerleaders began their antics again. The local audience had heard enough of their shrieking, their flailing arms and glimpses of tanned thighs and coloured panties. He stood at the edge of the circle and lifted the massive weight of the caber with hardly a grunt. It was only as the crowd quietened in expectation and the cheerleaders went silent, that Archie became aware of a quiet buzzing above him.

The swarm of bees, though only perhaps about two hundred strong, had escaped, enraged, from their broken home. They had risen high above the grass field of the games arena and could see no place where they could find rest. Perhaps resin has a particular attraction for bees. However, they were drawn towards this upwards stretching pole on the edge of the field and lead by their queen, they settled half way up its length.

The bees were invisible to all except for Archie. Archie hated bees, wasps and all stinging insects. Anaphylactic shock had killed a cousin of his in his youth and Archie had developed a morbid fear of the insects.

Archie was possessed of the combined need to give a winning performance with this throw and to get rid of these bees. He turned in the circle, balancing the caber, ready to toss, and then the instinct to flee took over. Instead of releasing the caber into the air, he began to run with it, away up the field.

The audience were incredulous.

"What's he doing, show off?"

"He can't be content with turning in the circle, he's got to run around with it first."

"Canadian show off, go back where you came from!"

Archie got half way down the field before he realised what he had done. He turned round and started to run back again. The audience were going wild. Shouting all sorts of curses and obscenities. Beer cans and empty cups were being rained down upon the gobsmacked cheerleaders, whose cries of "A R C H I E – A R C H I E" were growing more and more feeble.

Yukio was shouting and sobbing; he believed that he was being robbed of the opportunity to compete for honour to his people and honour for his ancestors. He went to where his robe and equipment was and drew out a long sword.

Archie came closer to the circle and the stand and now running at full pelt. He could see Yukio in front of him with the drawn sword and at the last moment he launched the caber, which flew up and into the stand, crashing through it next to the clan chief.

Archie stopped still. He knew he was in disgrace. Yukio rushed towards him with his drawn sword. It was only the foresight of another competitor in raising another caber and putting it in front of Yukio that stopped Archie from being split in two.

Instead, Yukio tripped, the sword spun in front of him and lodged handle-first in the earth, and Yukio fell chest-first onto it.

The clan chief picked himself up, dusted himself down and cautiously made his way off the wrecked stand. His microphone was reconnected and he sadly announced the early closure of the games – the first time in 92 years of modern history. To onlookers, the remains of the audience in the stand behind him seemed to be paying no attention at all but swatted each other with their programmes or stood up and performed their own little self-indulgent jigs with shakes of their heads. The cheerleaders were for some reason all pulling their skirts tight against their legs and also engaged in some new, absurd individual dance that involved them flailing around with their arms and kicking out with their legs.

The pipers were called on. Lead by the Dumbarton miniature pipers, they passed the stand, but no one except the drummers seemed to be playing. The pipers, red of face, appeared to be blowing and inflating their bags but to no effect. Then suddenly, all at once, the pipes groaned and the drone sticks burst with clouds of bubbles that rose gently in the breeze. The crowd burst into spontaneous applause; they had not seen this done before. The clan chief could only salute with a jaw that sagged low.

Somewhere in the crowds, Freddie and Irving were grinning. Bill was counting the cash from the stall and at the far end of the arena a small army of stall-holders were using extinguishers to put out an unexplained fire in the main catering tent.

CHAPTER 6

THE CALLAGHANS REMAINED oblivious of what had taken place in Mr Alexander's tent until that evening. Mr Alexander came round to see if the boys were alright and to explain to Mr and Mrs Callaghan that they had only done what could be expected since they had been outnumbered. Despite the damage done to his display, he had made more than ever before from honey sales. This would easily cover a replacement frame. Also, some kind souls, probably from the committee, had made a donation of a whole range of grocery and household goods which had been left in his van.

The Callaghans seemed shocked as they were told exactly what had happened. They, too, had been among the spectators when Archie had apparently gone raving mad, and poor Yukio had died in such a grisly fashion. It was going to be the talk of the area for some time to come. They were just glad that the boys had not seen the gruesome end.

By way of compensation Mr Alexander was offering to take the boys to the Naval headquarters at Faslane to see a nuclear submarine and perhaps even the opportunity to observe some target practice on Loch Long. The Callaghans thanked Mr Alexander; they were sure that the boys would be interested in the visit. They would ask them and phone him later in the evening.

The lads were out in the garden and had moved down well out of earshot and sight of the house. Bill turned to his brothers.

"I've counted out the money. Apart from what we're going to give back to Hamish, there is about forty pounds left over for us. That should be more than enough to get us out of here and back home south."

"About time too," said Irving. "Even though Alexander has forgiven me for the bees, I don't think that there's going to be a job there anymore."

"And," said Freddie, "we're going to have the Glasgow boys back on us again if we stay around here."

"We're agreed then?" asked Bill. "We wait till the morning and then set off home. We get the bus to Glasgow and then see if we can get a train or bus back down south."

George had puzzled over the guard's phone call. At first he had been worried that not only were the boys were in trouble again but that they could also be at risk. But then, he thought, the guard would have to go through the Callaghans. He was unlikely to tackle the boys on his own, and the Callaghans would not let him throw his weight around. Also George was hampered by the fact that his contacts, although they spread far and wide in England, did not really extend over the border into Scotland. He did not want to worry Mum and he could not leave her alone while he went off to sort out the trouble. The only solution he could think of was to make a visit to Scotland with Mum. A quick visit to check on the kids and for her to see her cousin.

Yes, that was obviously the solution. He began to make arrangements and hoped that Mum could take a couple of days off work.

The guard had actually arrived in Helensburgh on the morning of the games. He called at the address in Ederline Drive but got no answer. Making his way into the town, that seemed to be deserted as well. Quite a few shops had closed early or were not opening at all. He soon found out from a passer-by about the Highland games at Luss and caught a bus over there. He had paid his entrance fee and had just taken his place on the stand in time to see Archie's solo performance and Yukio's apparent ritual death. It was all over in fifteen minutes, and the crowd started to pour out. He kept his eyes open for the boys but the volume of people was just too great.

After waiting an hour, he decided that he needed to find a place to stay overnight before calling on the Callaghans again the next day.

Just before nine o'clock the boys were called in for a drink. It was usual for them to take this at the kitchen table with just Mrs Callaghan around. After a few minutes Mr Callaghan put his head around the door.

"Mr Alexander called round earlier this evening."

The boys looked up, expecting a telling-off to follow.

"He seems pleased with you despite the fight that took place with the Glasgow lads. It seems that he blames them entirely for what took place. Anyway, as a sort of reward, or compensation, I don't know which, he has invited you over to see the Naval base at Faslane. The latest nuclear submarine, *Resolution*, is there and you might even get a look over it, plus the chance to see some torpedo testing on Loch

Long. What do you think?"

"It sounds great," said Bill at once. "When is it planned for?"

"I'm not sure," said Mr Callaghan, "but I expect it will start in the morning. I have to ring Mr Alexander back if you are interested."

"Yes, we're interested," said Bill nodding towards his brothers in confirmation.

"Too right," said Freddie.

"Are they laying on food?" asked Irving.

"Aye lad, I'm sure there will be food; the Navy are not likely to let a meal break go past."

Agreed, the boys went up to bed.

Freddie whispered, "We will have to change our plans then?"

"Yeh," said Bill. "We'll see how the day goes on and take our opportunity when it comes."

That same evening Lester and Marcia Stellings were reunited in the village of Cardross, on the Clyde. Lester had been painstakingly visiting each town and village on the route out of Glasgow. He had stopped in Bishopton and stayed in Dumbarton overnight. On arrival in Cardross he had asked around about the boys and had visited the ruins of Cardross castle, where Robert the Bruce was supposed to have died.

Waiting for a change of buses later in the day, he could hardly believe his eyes as his daughter stepped down from a bus that was returning from Helensburgh. Marcia was in tears; Lester was in tears.

"What are you doing up here?" demanded the incredulous Lester.

Marcia continued to sob. "I came to find you, Dad. I couldn't stand it at home. Mum was making me clean everything; she wouldn't give me a break."

Lester consoled her. "How on earth did you find me then?"

Marcia explained how she had seen the phone message from Glasgow and how the receptionist had pointed her towards Helensburgh. But she had tried all the hotels and guest houses around Helensburgh; they were all full, but nobody had heard of her father. So she had left and was on her way back to Glasgow. She was so relieved that she had found him.

Lester knew about the games at Luss and that a lot of people used the hotels in Helensburgh to stay in. He explained to his daughter that they would either have to travel back to Glasgow to find rooms or go further north.

Marcia was willing to go anywhere as long as it was with her Dad and Lester was not quite finished with his Scottish adventure, so they decided to take a bus through to Arrochar where there was a hotel on the loch-side.

Breakfast had been taken. Irving was wiping a third slice of bread around his breakfast plate to get the last remains of egg and sauce. Mrs Callaghan waited patiently for him and added his plate to the others, piled so that they could be transferred to the sink. Irving greedily gurgled down the last drops of tea in his mug and then the three left the room to get coats on for the day.

Mr Alexander arrived at eight thirty to take them across to Faslane. Mrs Callaghan had insisted that they wore their smartest clothes for the visit. They pulled away from the house waving to Mr and Mrs Callaghan, who were relieved at the thought that the boys would be the responsibility of the Navy for the day and therefore little would go wrong. Mrs Callaghan had received a call from George on behalf of her cousin saying that they were coming up to visit. Mrs Callaghan had insisted that they stay at the house, but George wanted some space and some privacy and told her that she had enough on her hands with the boys, and that they would stay somewhere nearby.

As Mr Alexander's van passed out through Helensburgh, the remains of a recently burnt out derelict shop still smouldered. The boys took this in. Torchy was obviously still in the vicinity.

They drove up out on the route that they had taken the previous night. The scenery looked completely different in full daylight. After a half-hour drive they arrived at the tall gates of Faslane, the Clyde Naval Base.

A couple of military policemen came out of their hut. One took a sheaf of papers from Mr Alexander and poked his nose in through the window to take in the boys. The other started to go round the van with a mirror on a long silver rod.

"What's he playing at?" asked Freddie of everyone in the van.

"He's checking for bombs or something hidden underneath," said Mr Alexander. "Remember, this is a nuclear submarine base; they won't let anyone in. You're very privileged to be allowed to visit. Most of the locals don't get near the place."

Lieutenant Commander Spring was not having a good start to his day. He had arrived early to his office at seven thirty in order to get some work done undisturbed, and had just sat down at his desk with a cup of coffee when the phone rang. The Ministry of Defence was on the line. This was unheard of. These people never usually got into the office before ten o'clock. However, some bright young thing, with a posh South Kensington accent, was informing him that there were to be two additional high-status guests attending the torpedo testing that afternoon.

Damn and blast. He had worked hard preparing the schedule in fine detail two days ago. The pick-up from Glasgow airport, the reception lunch at the base, a tour of the base, a glimpse of *Resolution* and then off to Loch Long for the test firings, afternoon tea and then back to the airport. It seemed simple, but there was security to organise and transport, not to mention the catering. These flat-heads in London didn't have a clue.

On top of that he had promised his uncle that he would give some kids a tour. Now that would have to go out of the window. They could come some other day when he had time.

He took out his thin phone book and dialled the local number. Damn and blast again. No answer. Where was the silly old fool? He could not have set off already, surely?

In fact Mr Alexander was already in town filling up his van with petrol. Either his petrol consumption had shot up or the gauge was wrong. He had filled up just the other evening, before the games, and had only made a couple of journeys, and now it was nearly empty again!

Lieutenant Commander Spring got on with the changes in the arrangements for the day. The next thing he knew the phone was ringing again. It was the officer at the main gate.

"Your visitors have arrived, sir."

"Visitors, what visitors? Nobody is due until midday."

"No sir, not official visitors. Three lads with a permit to visit."

"Double damn and blast!" Despite the call to his uncle he had already forgotten about them.

He thought fast. Who can I assign them to so I can get out of this? It can't be any old person or it will get back to my uncle. Then he had a moment's inspiration. That young Wren officer that he had been introduced to last week. On secondment from Portsmouth. She had been given a full introduction to the base and would already know her way around. She would be ideal with three young kids. Ideal.

He got on the phone again and put a call through to the mess where she would probably be having breakfast.

"Lieutenant Eagling."

"Lieutenant Commander Spring. I have a favour to ask of you."

"Yes sir?"

"Can you get across to the main gate pronto and welcome some young visitors to the base? Get them some breakfast and then give them the guided tour."

"Of course, sir."

Thus it was Lieutenant Eagling who made her way across the parade ground to welcome the young lads to the base.

Mr Alexander had already driven off. He had thought that he might see his nephew, but he knew that he had an important job to do.

Lieutenant Eagling was not at her best with young kids, but she knew that she was doing her boss a favour and that she needed to put a bit of enthusiasm into things.

She approached the gate and put on a greeting smile. She could see the one gangly, and two other boys of a similar height looking inquisitively and expectantly towards her.

"Hello boys," she said. "I hear that Mr Alexander has arranged for you to be shown round the base. Welcome aboard HMS *Neptune*."

The boys looked at one another, puzzled. "We're not aboard any ship yet," said Freddie.

Lieutenant Eagling's smile shifted slightly, but stayed in place. "All Naval establishments are treated as vessels even though they are on land; then life goes on as if we were at sea."

"It sounds a strange thing to do," said Freddie.

"Don't start a row," said Bill. "Thanks very much. What do we call you?"

"Well, we'll drop formalities for the day. You may call me Jayne, and you are?"

"I'm Bill," said Bill. "This is Freddie," – he jerked his thumb towards Freddie – "and this is Irv."

"Pleased to meet you all," said Jayne.

"Now before we begin our tour I expect that you would like some breakfast?"

Before Bill could say that they had eaten, Irving gave him a hard kick on the shins and interrupted. "Yes, thanks very much."

"Jolly good. Well we'll go over to the officers' mess and see if there is still food on." They walked across the parade ground area and into an older building and up some steps.

It all seemed very posh to the boys. Everything was polished wood and brass. They were lead towards a large room.

"This is the officers' mess," explained Jayne.

Just outside, on either side of the doors were two giant glass and wood cases that contained fully rigged models of old sailing ships.

"Cor, what are these?" demanded Freddie.

Jayne stopped proudly before the one on the left. "This is the model of the original HMS *Neptune*, launched in 1683, and the other," Jayne indicated to the right, "is a model of the original HMS *Resolution* which was launched as the Tredagh in 1654, and renamed the *Resolution* in 1660. They are our pride and joy."

The three boys looked at the ships' details with genuine interest and fascination.

"Anyway," said Jayne, "go on in and sit down at one of the tables, and the orderly will get you anything that you need."

They sat down at a corner which was laid out with a linen tablecloth and silver cutlery. There were other officer types, ones and twos at tables. They glanced across at the boys but did not appear to take a lot of notice.

Jayne did not sit down with them but pointed out a card on the table that showed the list of what was available for breakfast. Freddie and Bill could see Irving's eyes growing bigger by the second. He looked up at Jayne.

"What, you can have all this for breakfast?" he asked, incredulously. First the kippers with Mr Callaghan, then the bee-keeping. Freddie and Bill could now see Irving signing up for the Navy on the spot.

"You make a selection," said Jayne. "Start with some porridge and then go onto a cooked breakfast. That's the norm."

The orderly came across to take their requests. Freddie and Bill just ordered porridge, but Irving could not help himself, and after porridge and toast, ordered a full Scottish breakfast with a kipper thrown in.

"Wouldn't sir rather have his kipper served on its own plate?"

"No bother," said Irving, "just chuck it all on the same plate. It'll save on the washing-up."

"Of course, sir, how thoughtful," said the orderly with the slightest of glances at Jayne.

Jayne left the boys to breakfast while she chatted with a couple of officers on an adjacent table.

While they ate their porridge, Freddie turned to his brothers. "Do you get the impression that we are not really wanted?"

"Yep, I think we've been off-loaded," said Bill. "Jayne seems as about as interested in taking us around here as a safe blower invited to a copper's promotion party."

"Yeh," said Irving. "I think we are going to have to make our own entertainment. At the first opportunity we'll ditch her."

The boys finished their meal. Irving finishing not long after the other two despite the feast before him. Jayne led them down a corridor to another large room set out with a screen, rather like a theatre.

"This is our briefing room," said Jayne. "I am going to tell you a bit about the history of the base and its role and then you will see a short Navy film about our surface and submarine fleet."

The boys settled down in the comfy seats and Jayne pulled down a chart in front of the screen and began droning on about facts and figures, strategic location and Political Geography. The boys eyes began to close after the first few minutes and then Jayne went to the rear of the room to start the film.

No sooner than it had started than Jayne said, "I'm just going out for a moment."

Bill nudged Irving and Freddie fully awake. "This is our chance."

Leaving the film showing the bows of warships plunging through heavy seas to strains of martial music, they dashed out the same way as Jayne had gone.

Fortunately one of the first things that Jayne had shown them was a plan of the base so that the boys had a rough idea of where they were going. They went out of the old building onto a higher level, which again was a large training area with a set of large shed doors on the opposite side. Some of these were open but there did not appear to be anyone around.

"It must be tea break or something," said Bill.

"Let's go and have a recce," said Irving.

They crossed the area and went into one of the shed doors. They then remembered what Jayne had said about the base being like a small town, even with its own fire brigade. Inside the shed were several army green fire engines. Lots of equipment was laid out in rows beside them but there was no sound of footsteps or voices. Freddie clowned around trying on one of the fireman's hats. Irving and Bill laughed as it slid down to cover most of his head down to his shoulders.

"Come on," said Irving. "There must be something more interesting than this."

"Hang on a minute," said Freddie. He had spotted a set of hoses and hydrant stopcocks to one side.

"You know what Jayne said about this being a ship?"

"Yeh," said Bill, "what of it?"

"Well," said Freddie, "then there's a distinct lack of water about."

Irving looked up. He could see what Freddie had in mind.

"I see what you mean, very dry for a ship."

"You two are off your heads," said Bill.

"Come on," said Freddie, "just a little drop."

Irving and Freddie went over to the hoses, stretched them out so that they faced out of the sheds and together turned the hydrants on. A wide spout of water surged out of the hoses and slicked across the training area and rapidly began to deepen as it reached the steps up to the officers' mess on the other side.

The boys moved off in the other direction, but before they disappeared into another area of the base, Freddie stopped them.

"Hey bruvs, you know those models back at the mess?"

"Yeh," said Irving. "I was having the same idea too."

"Oh, no you don't," said Bill.

But before he could do anything Irving and Freddie were away. As they finally left the scene, the two models were slowly being lifted from their stands by the rising waters.

Jayne had smoked two cigarettes. Damned kids. But, she thought, I had better go back in. She looked at her watch. Three more minutes for the film to run. She went back into the theatre where the film still flashed between sailors swivelling deck gun turrets into position and bows crashing through waves. A voice declaimed in strident Pathé News tones.

Where were the kids?

Her eyes were still adjusting to the gloom. Perhaps they had moved seats?

The film finished and the lights came back up. The theatre was definitely empty. Where the hell had they gone to?

Jayne had a sickening, sinking feeling in her stomach. Something was going very wrong and she was going to be held responsible. She raced back to an office at the end of the corridor and picked up the phone. But who was she going to call? If she phoned base security, there would be a general alert and she would immediately be to blame for the furore that would cause. They were only three kids. They wouldn't get far without an escort. All she had to do was to remain calm and search for them in an organised and logical manner.

She went back into the corridor and up to the door that led to the upper training ground. It was unlikely that they had back-tracked. They must have gone this way. It was then that she noticed that the carpet underfoot felt very mushy, almost as if it was wet. She opened the door to the training area and a surge of water a few inches deep rushed down the corridor.

Jayne peered out onto the, now clear, expanse of water. The light wind ruffled the surface and sent the model ships scurrying across the glinting lagoon, sails billowing and pennants streaming. One or two disenchanted seabirds that had come to claim the new water for themselves cast distrustful glances at their new nautical companions and squawked when they swept close by.

From the far side, in the sheds she could hear yelling.

"Get those bloody pumps on!" "Open up the drains!"

Oh hell, she thought. What a day for an incident like this. I hope the kids haven't got themselves soaked.

The three lads had made their way undetected all the way down to the waterside installations and there they had spotted the unmistakable silhouette of *Resolution*, its matt black hull, tall sail with winged diving planes making it look like some beached, malevolent whale.

They walked alongside it. Silent for once, in awe at the proportions of the vessel. They had stood there perhaps for several minutes before they heard rapidly approaching footsteps.

"Hey, you kids, what are you doing here?"

They turned to see an officer, quite highly ranked by the looks of all his gold bands.

"We're on a visit," said Bill. "We're being shown around but we seem to have lost our escort."

The officer looked doubtful. "This is a high security area. Technically you should have got nowhere near here without the proper authorisation."

"Just shows how careful you have to be," said Irving. "We could have been Russian spies."

"Yes, well. Even the Russians don't usually send in twelve-year-olds to do their work," he said with a twinkle in his eye. "If you tell me who was escorting you, we can track them down and reunite you."

The officer lead them away from *Resolution* and down to a small brick building about four hundred yards away.

"Wait here while I make a phone call."

The lads stood outside the building. There was a lot more activity just here with sailors going to and fro and a small crane was unloading from a vessel alongside. A large, open crate was dropped down nearby. The lads walked over to see what it was. The crane operator and two officers were looking into the crate.

"What's in there?" enquired Freddie.

"Torpedoes," said the officer. "They have just been shipped up from Coulport. These are the ones that are going to be used for the test firings this afternoon."

The boys peered into the crate at the different shaped torpedoes in the crate.

"They are all different," said Bill. "I thought they all looked the same."

"That's what the test firings are for," said the officer. "Different torpedoes work in different ways. We want to buy the best ones to suit our ships and submarines."

"So what's different then, apart from the shape?"

"All sorts of things. The explosive charge, the propulsion system, guidance system. Every one can have different internal workings."

"So guidance then?" asked Freddie, thinking, some deep memory being awakened within his brain. "How are these things usually guided?"

"It varies," said the officer. "Some use sonar. They home into the noise of the vessel they are attacking. Some use wire and they all use electromagnetic gyroscopes to keep them steady when they are launched."

"Aha," said Freddie, "I had read somewhere that they used gyroscopes."

He stretched his hand deep into his coat pocket and withdrew the magnets he had taken from the old radio set days ago. As the officers and the crane driver turned away, at the approach of the senior officer returning from the building, Freddie slipped them onto the nose of one of the torpedoes within the crate. They attached themselves to it with a satisfying clunk.

"So what's going on here then?" said the senior officer. "I thought I told you lads to wait by the building."

"No harm done," said one of the junior officers. "They were just interested in seeing the torpedoes being unloaded."

"I bet they were, the latest young recruits of the KGB are these lads," he said with a twinkle in his eye.

"Well, we've found your escort, WRNS Lieutenant Eagling, and she's going to get you a brief tour over *Resolution*, but we're going to shake you down for cameras first."

A rather sheepish-looking Jayne Eagling came round the corner.

"Sorry, sir, but they cut themselves adrift from me in the film theatre."

"Well, no harm done, I suppose," said the senior officer. "I hear that there is a bit of a flood crisis up at the main building."

"Yes, it looks as though the stopcocks got left on after a fire drill and some wags have floated the mess room display ships. The water has got into the building. They are trying to clear it up before the Lieutenant Commander gets back with his VIPs. God help some poor sod otherwise."

During this exchange the lads started to take a particular interest in things away in the opposite direction.

The lads were taken aboard *Resolution*. They climbed backwards down the steps from the tower into the hull of the submarine. The air smelled strange; it had a sort of electric, ozone quality about it, and the light below seemed to be a bluish green. They were surprised to find that despite the enormous size of the outside, everything inside seemed to be so crammed together. Even the control centre, while very modern and high-tech, seemed to have very little space for all the crew who operated within it.

Because the submarine was not operational, the reactor had been shut down, and the power was being taken from the base. The consoles and screens were all alive and the crew on board seem to be running procedures through them. Jayne explained to the boys the different pieces of equipment. They we all eager to know what everything did and the crew aboard gave up their green-backed seats so that the lads could see what it was like to be at the controls.

They were shown the periscope and at one stage Freddie asked, "What's this lever for?"

"Don't touch that," exclaimed Jayne.

But it was too late. Freddie had already pulled it. A shrieking, raucous, metallic klaxon sounded throughout the vessel.

"Diving stations!"

"Diving stations!"

Despite the fact that the skeleton crew on board knew that they were in dock, they all threw themselves at the equipment and controls as if they were at sea. Crew away from the control centre bruised themselves and sprained muscles as they jumped into an automatic response to seal pressure doors.

Jayne had gone a pale green colour and had to apologise to the red-faced commander on board who had raced up from the torpedo room to find out what the hell was going on.

The rest of the tour took place in an embarrassed silence and half an hour later the four emerged at the top of the tower into the welcoming breeze coming down the loch from the sea.

"I can't believe," said Irving, "that they've even got bunks under the spare torpedoes. What would happen if one of those things came loose?"

"And why," asked Freddie, "do they call the toilets 'the heads'?"

"Well I can answer that one," said Jayne. "On the old wooden ships the toilets used to be right under the figurehead."

"Anyway, now we've got to get some transport up to Loch Long so we can see some test torpedoes being fired."

"That should be good," said Bill and Irving together.

"You're right, it should," said Freddie in a quieter voice.

Unbeknown to the others, Marcia and Lester, George and Mum, the guard and Torchy had all checked into Arrochar Hotel at different times. They had all been driven away from Helensburgh and other places at the southern end of Loch Lomond by the guests that remained from the Luss games.

Lester had explained to Marcia his real purpose for coming north. Marcia was all for continuing with the mission to hunt down the boys. She too still blamed them for all that had happened to her family. However, Lester had had a change of heart and no longer sought revenge. Scotland and his encounter with Torchy had softened his heart. Torchy had taught him that there was a lot worse in this world than three overzealous schoolkids and Scotland was the place where he wanted to live. It was away from the false life that he had become sucked into in London and Sussex. He felt that he could start a new life here. All he had to do was to persuade Cynthia.

The guard, although he had softened, still wanted his hour with the boys. He no longer wanted the vengeance he had at first sought, but he did not want the boys to think that he was just their stooge, particularly as the discipline hearing could go badly. Additionally the trip had given him time to think and he had phoned to get some union advice. They were going to send a legal representative to support him at the hearing. This made him feel a lot better. At last he had someone on his side. That evening he would go back into Helensburgh and revisit the Callaghans and the boys.

Mum was enjoying her first real holiday for years and George was such a gentleman. They had dined first class on the train on the way up and now they were in this lovely hotel with romantic views over the loch and fine food. It was as if she were on honeymoon again.

That evening they were going to visit her cousin and see the lads. She secretly really missed them all and could hardly wait for the few hours to pass.

Torchy was making the most of this hotel life. He still had a few pounds left from the wallet he had found in Carlisle. He had found the kids and returned the favour. The catering tent at Luss had been a bit of a failure. He had expected more of a blaze there, but the old shop in Helensburgh had gone up a treat. Now he was going to get a chance at a second hotel – this time, hopefully, without the interference of that fool that had stopped him at Glasgow.

Lieutenant Commander Spring had done his duties at Glasgow Airport. The MOD bods and military attachés had been greeted and collected and now they were all on their way back in an escorted convoy for lunch.

As soon as he entered the main building on the base at the head of the column of VIPs, he could tell that something was awry. It was much too warm and the air had a fetid, odd smell about it, like ... he was not sure – a dead rat or burned rug perhaps. He strode towards the mess room.

The first thing that he observed was that the two display cases were empty. His blood pressure began to rise. He started to get that throbbing sensation at the back of his neck. They knew that he loved to stop with his guests while he pointed out the detailed features on his beloved models. Who the hell had moved them? He marched, ill-tempered, into the room. It was lined with flunkeys and the table set with glasses, cutlery and china, as it should be.

They were all seated at their tables and the first course served. As the wine waiter hovered, filling his glass, Lieutenant Commander Spring caught his arm.

"What's going on? What's that smell?"

"Smell, sir?"

"Don't mess with me. The whole place stinks like someone's just died. What is it?"

"A flood, sir. The building got flooded from the hydrants in the training area, sir, and someone put the models out to sail."

"What!" the Lieutenant Commander almost shouted. The VIPs were beginning to look. The wine waiter's arm was being held so hard that he was wincing with pain and the wine was still pouring from the bottle and into an overflowing glass. "I'm going to have someone's guts for garters. Pass the message on: heads are going to roll, nobody's going to make a fool of me!"

It was a very bad-tempered Lieutenant Commander who joined the assembled group of VIPs and dignitaries on the viewpoint over Loch Long and the target range. He scanned the assembled party and as he caught sight of the smiling faces of Freddie, Bill and Irving, his neck started to throb again and a muscle beneath his right eye started to go into an involuntary spasm. He was just about to ask what the devil they were doing there when he realised that it had been part of the invitation issued to his uncle. He must pull himself together. They were only kids; they could have nothing to do with the debacle this day was turning in to.

The crowd took up positions at an array of mounted binoculars and telescopes that could swivel between the launching point and the target, which was the silhouette of a frigate attached to the hull of an old ship.

The firing was not to be done from a submarine but from specially constructed tubes mounted on a vessel designed so that the tubes fired from beneath the waterline. A tannoy announced that they were to see the firing of four different types of torpedo. All torpedoes contained an explosive charge for effect, but considerably less than in conflict use.

The target, although it stood still in the water, could be towed and produced the sound of a real frigate under power. The VIPs were informed that the torpedoes all included failsafe devices that could self-destruct the torpedo if it missed its target or if it should turn and try to re-engage the vessel that it had been launched from.

The lads were handed binoculars by Jayne and eagerly awaited the first launching. The tannoy announced that the first torpedo was a modified British Mark 23 torpedo, with wire guidance and target acquisition logic. They could see a burst of bubbles and the movement of the missile just below the surface as it moved towards the target.

Nothing happened. There was murmuring among the dignitaries as they were told that the command wire had been severed on launch and the torpedo run had automatically been deactivated.

Freddie had stayed with his binoculars trained upon the shape of the torpedo, struggling to remember the exact shape of the torpedo onto which he had put the magnets. Perhaps these had caused the problem. In that case this was going to be no fun at all.

The second firing was of an American Mark 48 torpedo with gyroscopic stabilisation and sonar sensors. The torpedo streamed towards its target and was within metres of it when it shot off course. The tannoy announced a guidance error and stated that now the missile would be destroyed by an onboard failsafe system. Nothing happened.

The boys looked up at the faces of the naval staff. There were the beginnings of concern. Someone was in short-wave radio contact with the firing base.

"The order for torpedo destruct has been given, sir, from firing control."

"Well, why hasn't it self destructed?"

"Send a failsafe destruct order."

"That has already been sent."

All eyes were on the torpedo trail. It had gone round behind the target, turned and was returning towards the firing base.

"That's impossible," said the Lieutenant Commander.

An American Naval commander had come to the radio.

"Re-enter the failsafe sequence, re-enter the failsafe sequence," he shouted into the mouthpiece.

"What do you think we've been doing," came back the reply in clipped English tones, "making a ruddy pot of tea?"

"It wouldn't happen with a British torpedo," the MOD observers were muttering.

"Typical of a Yankee torpedo not knowing when to stop."

"I blame the water up here," came back an American attaché. "The water here is far too cold. They did the testing in Florida."

Jayne looked at the boys. "There seems to be a problem."

The tannoy had gone silent. The boys looked at each other. Then Bill and Irving looked at Freddie.

"You didn't ....?" asked Irving.

Freddie held up his hands. "They were only small magnets."

There was the beginning of panic in the voice of the Lieutenant Commander. "That torpedo is still travelling and it has a live warhead."

"It's circling, sir."

"What do you mean?"

"It's going in circles around the target."

"If it goes on as it is, it's going to strike the shore on one side of the loch or the other."

"Well, what is there to hit?"

"Well, sir, on one side woods and trees. On the other, a hotel."

George and Mum were sitting on the veranda of the hotel in the warm sun. Each of them had a drink in their hand. They looked across at the target site and could see the firing point away down the loch.

"What a beautiful place," said Mum. "The land of the mountain and the flood," said George. Their glasses chinked together.

"I wonder what the boys are doing now? I can't wait to see them this evening."

Two more guests walked out. Lester and Marcia sat down with drinks at a table some distance from George and Mum. George looked up and peered hard at Lester. He tapped Mum on the arm.

"Isn't that Lester Stellings over there, with his daughter?"

Mum looked across. "It certainly looks like them. What in heaven's name are they doing up here?"

Lieutenant Commander Spring had the other British naval officers around him.

"If the torpedo hits near the hotel, there are going to be casualties."

"We have only got a matter of minutes. We cannot stop the torpedo."

"It's fifteen minutes by road to the hotel. We have no way of warning them."

"The short-wave radio only links with the firing base. We have no phone contact."

The lads had moved over with Jayne into earshot.

"Isn't the hotel nearly beneath us on this hill?" asked Bill.

"More or less," said the Lieutenant Commander, "but it's a sheer drop."

The boys moved over to the edge. It was very steep, but there were trees and craggy outcrops rather than a straight fall.

Bill turned to the Lieutenant Commander. "We can get down there and raise the alarm."

"You're not going down; it's too dangerous. Anyway, the torpedo may not strike this side."

"Maybe it will," said Bill. "Have you got any ropes?"

One of the officers turned. "I'm sure there are some in the jeep."

Irving sprinted over, pulled a coil of rope out of the back and before the officers could prevent them, they had tied off the rope and they were over the edge.

Once they were over the first fall, the descent was quite easy. They went from trees to crags of rocks and back to trees. They were down in a few minutes. They ran to find the entrance of the hotel and there before them were sitting their Mum and George. There was no time for surprise, no time for re unions.

"You've got to get out," yelled Bill. "There's a stray torpedo on the loose."

"What?" said George.

"Freddie, Bill, Irving, what ever is going on?" asked Mum.

Freddie and Irving grabbed their hands and dragged them behind the hotel. Marcia and Lester recognised the boys and could hear the urgency in their voices. They followed them to the safety behind the hotel. Bill flew into the hotel entrance and struck the fire alarm on the wall opposite the reception desk. He shouted to the stunned receptionist to get everyone out.

Upstairs the guard heard the bell. Bloody fire drills, he thought. I'm not moving. He returned to his bed and pulled up the cover.

Torchy was already at work, laying his trail of gasoline away from the central heating boiler. This one is going to go up big, he thought. This time there will be no distractions.

Most of the guests were behind the hotel when they torpedo struck. Even the limited high explosive sent rocks and bricks flying high into the air. The windows of the hotel flew inward as the shock wave hit them. Bits of roof masonry fell down and wooden beams cracked.

The shaking of the building caused Torchy to stumble on the stairs as he had lighter and petrol can in his hands. He fell down the stairs with the lit lighter and petrol pouring from the can. He became a human torch and, screaming, tried to make his way up the stairs while flailing away at the flames that were starting to engulf him.

The explosion had thrown the guard up into the air and onto a hard, cold floor. He rubbed his eyes and walked shakily towards the window. He looked out the window and saw tiles still falling. He could smell smoke. He heaved the sash window up and saw the long drop down to the ground. He began shouting for help.

The lads heard his shouts and ran towards his calls. The guard looked as the footsteps came closer, then as the boys drew into sight he rubbed his eyes. Was this real or a nightmare? However, before he could decide, Irving had the rope off his shoulder. He had recognised the guard.

"Hoi Goebbels, catch the rope."

The rope was in the air and the guard did as he was told. He caught the end and tied it to his bedstead. The three lads, all grinning, watched him gingerly edge his ample bottom out over the windowsill and then down on the rope.

As the echoes of the explosion died away from the surrounding hills, the boys and the guests went round to the front of the hotel to inspect the damage. As they reached the front door, a smoking, yelping figure emerged into view.

Lester immediately recognised him.

"It's that madman from Glasgow, Deggey. He's an arsonist."

Hotel staff doused Torchy down with water from a hose and stood around him waiting for the authorities and ambulance to arrive.

The boys led the still staggering but grateful guard to the front of the hotel. There George and Mum stood observing the scene.

"I suppose that it would be the wrong time to ask if you boys know anything about why our hotel has been on the receiving end of a naval torpedo?" asked George.

Freddie, Bill and Irving looked at George with puzzled expressions. George held their glances for a second or two longer than he needed to. Mum stepped forward and planted a sticky kiss upon each of them in turn, along with a fond hug

EPILOGUE

LESTER AND MARCIA returned that evening to Glasgow Central hotel. Marcia had told Lester of the message from the receptionist. The hotel manager thanked Lester for his actions. He had saved the hotel from a major fire. In return the hotel wanted to offer the post of hotel safety officer to Lester, if he was willing to do that sort of work.

Cynthia did not take a lot of persuading and within months they were living on the outskirts of Helensburgh. Lester now sleeps well and Marcia soars above the world again in her dreams.

Mr Roberts, the guard, did not lose his job but was asked to transfer to the Eastern Division, where he works on the service between Norwich and Liverpool Street.

Lieutenant Commander Spring awarded the boys a special citation for bravery. They were invited to a ceremony on the base three months later with their family. Mrs Callaghan was there wearing a new red hat. Mr Callaghan wore his bottle-green waistcoat beneath his donkey jacket.

Freddie was overheard remarking that last time they had been on board, the ship had sprung a leak. This brought about a long and hard stare from the Lieutenant Commander. On his desk, too, was a forensic report that had found unexplained magnetic material on the remains of the torpedo body, which was both a mystery to the designers and the manufacturers.

After several months in a burns unit, Torchy went to trial and received an eighteen year sentence. He was released from Brixton Prison in 1981. He walked out of the gate on a warm August morning. He looked down towards the town and could see smoke rising from the riots that were underway in the town centre. Torchy jumped on a bus to take him into the chaos, in the mistaken belief that celebrations for his release were already underway.

The boys returned to their home town in late August as heroes and set up their stall by the pier, which now included large supplies of Highland honey for sale.

George lives with Mum in their home and every afternoon pops in to see Mum on the pier. He always comes away with a smile upon his face and a twinkle in his eyes.

ISBN 142517692-5